APPLE 🍎 FANTASY

The Things with Wings

Gregory J. Holch

SCHOLASTIC INC.

New York   Toronto   London   Auckland   Sydney
Mexico City   New Delhi   Hong Kong

No part of this publication may be reproduced in whole or in part, or stored in a retrieval system, or transmitted in any form or by any means, electronic, mechanical, photocopying, recording, or otherwise, without written permission of the publisher. For information regarding permission, write to Scholastic Inc., Attention: Permissions Department, 555 Broadway, New York, NY 10012.

ISBN 0-590-93502-X

12 11 10 9 8 7 6 5 4 3   9/9 0 1 2 3 4/0

Printed in the U.S.A.   40

First Scholastic paperback printing, May 1999

The text type is New Aster.
Interior design by Kristina Iulo

FOR RHONDA

CONTENTS

"...TWO CATERPILLARS...WERE CRAWLING ALONG ON THE GROUND WHEN A BUTTERFLY FLEW OVER THEM. AND ONE CATERPILLAR SAID TO THE OTHER, 'YOU'LL NEVER CATCH ME GOING UP ON ONE OF THOSE'..."

—MADELEINE L'ENGLE

From her Smith College commencement
address entitled "To Ride a Butterfly" (1977)

The
Things
with
Wings

1.

THE EMERALD RAINBOW

Every year, on the first warm, sunny day of
spring, the butterflies returned to the little
town of Angel Falls.

In the same way that the swallows return each
spring to the town of San Juan Capistrano, or the
great flocks of millions of Monarch butterflies
travel each fall to a tiny four-acre valley in the
mountains of Mexico, the butterflies flew back to
Angel Falls.

No one seemed to know why they came. They
didn't stay long — only one week — before contin-
uing their migration north. But for that one week

each spring, the town was literally covered with the multicolored butterflies known as the Emerald Rainbow.

It was an afternoon near the end of April, during spring vacation, and Newton Bellnap was sitting under an apple tree in the middle of a field, waiting for the first butterfly of spring.

It had rained for twelve days and twelve nights without stopping, but this morning he had awakened to find that the sun was shining and that overnight the whole world had turned green.

Everywhere, leaves had appeared on the trees, leaves that were a bright, light, early spring "new green." It was his favorite color.

Spring was Newton's favorite time of year, and this was his favorite spot to come to when he wanted to get away from people and just think.

Newton was new in town. His parents were actors and were always on the move, but this time they said they were putting down roots.

It was a little noisy at home right now. His mother and father were roaming the house practicing their lines out loud for a movie, and his brothers and sisters added to the background noise. So Newton had been happy to find this quiet spot that he could call his own.

He was sitting with his back against the apple tree. Because the ground was still damp from the rain, he had stretched his legs out along the exposed roots of the tree. It was hard to tell where the roots ended and his legs began. Around him stretched a carpet of white apple blossoms that had fallen from the tree above.

He had a book in his lap, *Ten Great Mysteries* by Edgar Allan Poe, but he wasn't really a reader. The book was something he had to read for Mrs. Forest's English class. No . . . Newton thought of himself more as a "movie person." He'd seen *The Pit and the Pendulum* and *The Murders in the Rue Morgue* a couple of times each on TV. He was hoping that if the stories turned out to be close enough to the movies, he would be able to sneak by without actually having to read too much Poe.

A warm gentle breeze had sprung up from the west, and Newton took off his jacket, sighing happily. On top of everything else, it was Monday afternoon, and there was no school for a week. It was a perfect day. He wished that time would just stand still and his life could stay like this forever.

It wasn't the first time he'd had a thought like that. As much as he liked the changes that spring brought each year, he didn't really like it when things changed. He didn't know exactly why he felt that way. Maybe it was because his family was always moving.

Newton had arrived at his new school in the middle of the semester, and even there he'd noticed that things were changing. He had only just met some of the kids in his classes, but already he could see that something was happening to some of them. Their faces were getting thinner, more angular and serious looking ... "harder" was the way he thought of it. He didn't like it, and he didn't want it to happen to him.

Newton knew what he didn't want in life — he didn't want change. But what then did he want?

He thought about it for a minute and decided that a little adventure might be fun, as long as it didn't require a lot of effort, and of course, as long as he didn't have to change anything about himself.

He picked up his book and opened to the story, *The Purloined Letter*. It had something to do with a guy who hid a letter by leaving it out in plain sight. Newton didn't see how reading Poe would ever help him in real life, but he figured he might as well get the reading out of the way. Then his whole vacation would be free.

He looked at the first sentence, and just as he started to read, something fluttered down and landed smack in the middle of the page. At first Newton thought it was an apple blossom, but when he looked again, he saw that it was alive.

It was a butterfly — the first Emerald Rainbow butterfly of the year. Newton had been hearing about the butterflies ever since his family had moved to Angel Falls. The arrival of millions of butterflies, stopping in town for a week on their annual migration, was the biggest thing that happened in this town, and guessing the exact arrival date had become the number one topic of conversation for the past month.

Newton looked around the field, hoping to see more butterflies, but this was the only one in sight. Slowly, so as not to startle it, he lifted the book to get a closer look.

The butterfly was fairly large. It had a thin black body and a wing span about the width of Newton's hand. The top sides of its wings were the same light, bright, emerald green as the new leaves on the trees, but underneath, the wings were a rainbow swirl of colors. Newton knew that it was this combination of colors that gave the butterfly its name.

The butterfly flew off, and Newton prepared to read, but suddenly there it was again, alighting in the center of the book. He reached out to touch it, and the butterfly flew away, but a few seconds later it was back, landing again on the exact same spot in the middle of the first page of *The Purloined Letter*.

It stood there on its six legs and slowly opened and closed its wings: emerald, rainbow, emerald, rainbow, emerald. . . .

Newton sat there, trying to watch the butterfly, but his eyes would not stay open. Before he knew it, his head had tipped back against the tree, and he was fast asleep.

The warm spring breeze continued to blow gently across the field. It whispered past Newton's ears and caressed his hands until it looked as if the open book he held was full of flying pages. Perhaps it was the breeze, perhaps it was the book, or perhaps it was the butterfly, but Newton had the strangest dream.

In the dream, he was running down the same field in which he was now sitting. Away in the distance was something he had to get to, although he couldn't quite see what it was. He was running faster and faster, his eyes trying to see into the darkness of the woods at the edge of the field, when suddenly the ground beneath his feet ended. He looked down, but it was too late.

In front of him was a giant crack in the earth that looked as wide and as deep as the Grand Canyon. He hadn't seen it coming, and now his momentum carried him over the edge, and he found himself falling headfirst through emptiness, into a place that was gray and cold.

Down, down, down he fell, until he was about to hit the bottom.

"I'm going to crash," he thought.

And just at that moment something struck him on the head, and he woke up.

"What?" he said, sitting up straight, still half in the dream.

Newton looked around. His book had slid from his hands, and the butterfly was gone, but beside the book, on the ground, was an apple. It was green and almost ripe, which was odd, since this was spring, and there wouldn't be apples on the tree until fall. Newton picked it up to examine it. The apple had a little dent in the side that marked where it had hit him, and near the bottom was a small oval sticker with a price on it and the words: CERTIFIED ORGANIC.

Newton heard a rustling sound above him and looked up.

There, looking down at him through the leaves and apple blossoms was the face of a girl. She stared at him for a few seconds, then she spoke.

"It's about time," she said. "Wake up! There are things to do."

2.

THE GIRL IN THE TREE

Newton looked at the face framed among the blossoms. He'd seen that face before, he was pretty sure.

Then he remembered. It belonged to a girl in his science class in school. He didn't really know her. She sat in the back by the windows. She was the one who'd pointed out rather loudly in class that the teacher had hooked up the batteries the wrong way in a science experiment. It had something to do with connecting positive terminals to negative terminals, not positive to positive. She'd been right, too.

Suddenly the girl let out a shriek and fell backward out of sight.

Newton jumped to his feet, only to find the girl hanging upside down by her knees from a branch, her upside down eyes now staring in a direct line into his.

"Come on up, the air's fine," said the girl.

"Uhh, no thanks," said Newton. Perhaps he spoke a little too quickly, because the girl asked, "You're not afraid of heights, are you?"

Actually, Newton was afraid of heights, but he simply replied, "I prefer to keep my feet on the ground."

The girl nodded. "You're Newton Bellnap, aren't you? You run the machines when we see a film in science class. I'm Vanessa. Vanessa Zephyr."

"Yes, I know," said Newton, trying to sound polite. He realized that even though he saw her every day in school, he hadn't known her name at all.

Vanessa climbed back into the tree, disappearing for a moment.

"Catch!" she called from somewhere among the blossoms, and a second later a green teardrop-shaped backpack came hurtling at him. Newton caught it — just barely. It was so heavy, he nearly dropped it.

"What have you got in here?" he asked.

"Oh, a little bit of this and a little bit of that. I like to be prepared," said the voice from the tree.

Suddenly there was a loud thrashing noise, and Vanessa came plummeting through the leaves and branches, her arms flailing and flapping furiously, and hit the ground with a "thud" that Newton could feel in the soles of his feet.

"Are you all right?" he asked, running over to where Vanessa had fallen.

"Of course I'm all right!" she said, standing and brushing herself off. "Why don't you just forget you ever saw that."

Newton didn't know if she was serious or joking. It had almost looked as if she'd been trying to fly.

"I didn't see anything," said Newton, finally. "Except you falling out of the tree."

"Thank you," she said and then paused. "This is going to sound silly," she continued, "but when I was younger, I used to think I might be able to fly if I could only flap my arms fast enough. It never worked. I know it seems totally immature, but every now and then, especially on a spring day like this, I still like to give it a try. Just in case."

She sat down and reached out for the backpack that Newton was still holding.

"I want you to take a look at something," she continued. "You're the audiovisual expert. Why is this broken?"

She reached into her pack and pulled out a thin plastic cartridge from which a long tangle of recording tape hung dangling.

"It's the tape cassette to our answering machine at home," said Vanessa. She handed it to Newton.

"It looks a little jammed," he said, smiling.

Vanessa grabbed the tape cassette and pulled it out of Newton's hands.

"You're laughing at me," she said. "Listen, I don't need your help. I don't need anyone's help with anything."

Newton looked at her for a moment.

"I wasn't laughing at you," he said quietly. "I was just thinking that you can get answering machines that do everything electronically. You don't have to worry about tape anymore."

"It's my father's machine," said Vanessa. "He just says, 'If it ain't broke, don't fix it.'"

Newton reached for the cassette and gently pulled it from her hands.

"What happened to it?" he asked.

"I was away all day, and when I got back last night I saw that there was a phone message. I started playing it back, and then this happened. Do you think it can be fixed?"

Newton turned the cassette over carefully a few times.

"I don't suppose you have a pen with you?" he asked.

Vanessa reached into her backpack, rummaged around a little, and pulled out a pen.

Newton took it and pushed it, clip-end first, into the hole on the take-up reel. When the pen was wedged into the hole, he started to spin it slowly. Little by little, the tangled mess of tape began to be drawn back into the cassette shell.

Vanessa pulled the cassette out of Newton's hands once more and finished the job herself.

"I did it!" she said. "I can't believe it was so easy. What made it get tangled?"

"How often do you clean the tape heads and capstan rollers on your answering machine?" asked Newton.

Vanessa gave him a blank look.

"What's a capstan roller?" she asked.

Newton sighed. "The tape will probably play now," he said.

To his surprise, Vanessa pulled out a tiny portable cassette player from inside her pack and snapped in the tape.

"It has a built-in speaker. We can both listen," she said.

The tape was silent for a minute. Then a voice spoke. It sounded faint and far away.

"Oh, Vanessa, why aren't you at home?" asked the voice. "I feel as if I'm F.T.P."

Vanessa stopped the tape.

"That's Ruth Ann Harbinger," she said. "Do you know Ruth Ann?"

Newton shook his head, no. There were two homerooms for his class at school, and she wasn't in his. She wasn't in any of his other classes, either.

"What does F.T.P. mean?" he asked.

"It's an abbreviation. Each letter stands for a word. She always talks like that. It means Falling To Pieces."

Vanessa started the tape again.

"It's my birthday," said the voice. "I've been sitting here waiting for hours, and no one has come to my party. Is this what it means to be twelve?"

There was a pause, then the voice continued.

"I wish I hadn't told my mother she could pick the guests for my own birthday party. Why do I always do things like that?"

There was another pause.

"I should have invited you, Vanessa. You would have come. You wouldn't have canceled at the last minute claiming you were sick the way most of the others did."

Silence.

"Something else . . ."

More silence.

"Something strange . . ."

There was a long pause, then Ruth Ann spoke in a voice so soft they could hardly hear it. "How did I get so tired? . . . Can't keep my eyes open. What's happening to me?"

There was a pause.

"Vanessa . . . I'm so sorry."

And that was all.

They waited a minute more, watching the tiny tape reels of the cassette turn round and round.

Finally, Newton spoke.

"Fast forward it," he said. "But keep the play

button pushed down. There might be more on the tape. I didn't hear her hang up the phone. It sounds like your answering machine kept recording."

Vanessa pushed the fast forward button.

"I don't think there's anything more," she said, and just then there was the high pitched burble of a voice from the tape player.

"Go back and play that at normal speed," said Newton.

Vanessa rewound the tape and pressed the play button.

A new voice spoke. Three words.

"It's happening again," said the voice. Then the line went dead.

3.

THE MAN IN THE BLACK HAT

"That was odd," said Newton. "Who was that last voice?"

"That was Ruth Ann's mother — Gabriella Harbinger," said Vanessa. "Ruth Ann and I used to be best friends. It was her twelfth birthday this past weekend. Our birthdays are just a few days apart. Usually we have one big party for the both of us, but this year she said she wanted her own party, and she didn't invite me."

"It almost sounded like she was trying to apologize," said Newton. "Maybe you should call her."

"I've got a better idea," said Vanessa. "She doesn't live far away. Let's go over there right now. I'm a little worried about her."

She grabbed her backpack, but Newton hesitated, glancing at his school book on the ground. He hadn't finished reading the Poe story, but then again, any excuse to postpone a school assignment was a good excuse. Besides, there was no real hurry. He had all spring vacation to read it.

"OK," he said. "Let's go."

He picked up his book and jacket, and Vanessa and he were just starting out, when they heard a noise that sounded like shouting.

The field was bordered by woods, and now out from the shadow of the trees on the far edge of the field stepped a man.

He was wearing a black wool baseball hat with a black leather brim, and silver mirrored sunglasses. The man had a small pack over one shoulder, and in his hands was a large butterfly net.

"Vanessa," the man called from the edge of the field. "Vanessa? Is that you?"

"Who's that?" Newton whispered to Vanessa.

"Oh . . . he's a professor at the local college," she

replied. "He's a little strange. Don't pay any attention to him. I don't."

The man came closer.

"Vanessa, it *is* you," he said as he walked up to them. "I thought I might find a fellow scientist like you out here on a day like this. I'm sure you know that the Emerald Rainbow butterfly migration is going to arrive any day now."

Vanessa turned to Newton and rolled her eyes.

"I just wanted to warn you," the man continued. "If you're looking for butterflies, stay in this field. Don't go into the woods. There are some strange diseases you can get from insects in the woods during the spring. Lyme disease and . . . well, other things. Stay in the field, and maybe you can help me with a special study I'm doing."

He opened the pack on his shoulder.

"This is a collecting jar," he said, turning to Newton and handing him something that looked like a large jelly jar. "Don't worry, it has holes punched in the top. You can put butterflies inside, and they'll still be able to breathe."

He pulled out a second jar and handed it to Vanessa.

"I'm prepared to pay you for each Emerald

Rainbow butterfly you collect. It won't be easy, they're fast."

"Isn't that one over there by the road?" asked Vanessa, pointing back toward one edge of the field.

"Where? Where?" asked the man. He turned abruptly, closing his pack. "Remember what I told you," he called over his shoulder. "Stay in the field. Don't go into the woods."

He practically shouted these last words, and then he raced off, his butterfly net waving in the direction Vanessa had pointed.

As soon as he was out of sight, Vanessa took her jar and flung it against the apple tree as hard as she could. It bounced off the tree, and she had to try three times before she finally broke it. Then she grabbed Newton's jar and shattered it, too.

"He makes me so angry sometimes," she said, her eyes intense with fury. "I would never put a butterfly in a bottle. If you ever see him again, don't tell him anything about butterflies. Not anything. At least if you want to be my friend. Promise me."

"I promise," said Newton.

"Cross your heart and hope to die . . ."

"Cross my heart and hope to die . . ."

"Stick a specimen pin in your eye . . ."

"Stick a specimen pin in my eye . . ."

"You will never hurt a butterfly."

"I will never hurt a butterfly."

"Good," said Vanessa. "Now let's go see Ruth Ann."

She started off, but Newton hung back.

"Maybe we should wait," he said. "I was sort of hoping to be here when the butterflies came."

"You won't see any butterflies today," said Vanessa.

"But I saw one already," said Newton.

"Then it was just an early scout. The butterfly migration won't get here until tomorrow morning."

"How do you know?" asked Newton.

"Trust me," she said. "I'm a scientist. I know just about everything there is to know about the Emerald Rainbow butterflies. I've been studying them ever since I was a little kid. Come on. Let's get out of here before that guy comes back."

4.

IF IT FLIeS, KiLL IT

Ruth Ann's mother was a woman of few words.

"Ruth Ann can't talk to you today," she said.

Then she pulled the screen door closed and shut the front door in their faces.

"This happens all the time," said Vanessa. "She thinks I'm a bad influence on her daughter. She says I have an overdeveloped imagination that's going to get me into trouble. I'm sure Ruth Ann is here. We'll just go around back and see what she has to say for herself."

There was a walk paved with gray flagstones

that led under the trees, and they followed it around to the back of the house.

"This will just take a minute," said Vanessa, reaching for the handle on the screen door. "We'll be out of here before her mother ever knows we were inside."

She pushed on the latch and tried to pull the door handle toward her. It didn't move. The door was locked.

Vanessa took a step backward.

"There's more than one way to skin a cat," she said.

With both hands she grabbed the low hanging branch of a tree that stood beside the house. Then she leaned back and swung both legs up between her arms and around and over the branch, so that she was hanging upside down by her knees. From there, she pulled herself into a sitting position, and then climbed up into the tree until she disappeared in the leaves near the upper windows of the house.

"I'll wait down here," Newton called up to her, but Vanessa didn't answer. He didn't know if she had heard him.

Newton walked up to the house and peered into the nearest window. He was looking into a room that appeared to be a sort of family room or den. The lights were out, but he could see well enough to notice that the walls were covered with framed photographs. The photos were all pictures of a little girl with a pink ribbon in her hair.

In the far corner of the room, a high backed leather chair faced the wall. Someone appeared to be sitting in the chair, but all that Newton could see was the back of their head.

Newton pushed his face against the window screen, trying to get a closer view. Was that Ruth Ann? He couldn't stop staring at her hair.

Above him, Newton could hear Vanessa tapping on the screen of one of the upstairs windows.

"Ruth Ann!" he heard her call. "Ruth Ann!"

A moment later, Vanessa climbed back down and dropped to the ground beside him.

"I was sure she'd be in her room," said Vanessa. "But I didn't see her."

"Maybe you were looking in the wrong room," said Newton.

"It was her room, all right," said Vanessa. "There isn't another room like it anywhere. Her mother painted it pink and filled it up with dolls and a giant dollhouse when Ruth Ann was little. She wanted Ruth Ann to keep it that way forever.

In fact, she still tries to make Ruth Ann wear a pink ribbon in her hair the way she used to when she was younger, and Ruth Ann does it to keep her happy. But Ruth Ann has this really dramatic artistic flair, and last year she talked her mother into letting her paint the ceiling of her room black. It was definitely not the wrong room."

"That's not what I meant," said Newton. "I meant maybe you should have looked down here. There's someone in there." He pointed to the ground floor window. "Only I have to warn you, there's something strange about whoever it is."

"Strange?" asked Vanessa. "What's strange?"

"It's their hair," said Newton. "It's green."

Vanessa took a minute to digest this piece of information.

"I want to know what's going on here," she said, and she marched off around the side of the house. Newton followed her to the front door.

Vanessa leaned on the doorbell.

"I'm not going until someone comes out and gives us an explanation," she said.

The doorbell was not a harsh buzzer, but a four-tone chime. However, repeated over and over again, it did have a certain urgency all its own.

Finally, there were footsteps from inside the

house, and once again, Ruth Ann's mother opened the front door. She looked at Newton and Vanessa. She opened her mouth to speak, but just then Vanessa pulled open the screen door, dodged around her, and dashed inside.

"Ruth Ann! Ruth Ann!" Vanessa called.

Mrs. Harbinger turned and charged after her, slamming the front door behind them both.

Newton stood outside the house, not sure what to do. He had just about decided to follow them, and was reaching for the handle on the screen door, when he noticed something caught between the screen door and the house door, its wings beating faintly against the screen.

It was another Emerald Rainbow butterfly. Or was it the same one he'd seen before?

The butterfly clung to the screen with its wings outstretched.

Newton pulled the screen door open, and tried to brush the butterfly gently away, but it would not let go.

"Butterfly, butterfly, fly away home," he said. "Your house is on fire, your children have flown."

It was a nursery rhyme he had learned when he was little. Had it actually been about butterflies? He couldn't remember.

He was standing there, trying to shake the butterfly loose from its hold on the screen door, when the front door opened and Mrs. Harbinger reappeared.

She took one look at the butterfly and let out a shriek. Newton stumbled backward, and the butterfly flew straight up past Mrs. Harbinger's head and off into the sky.

"Don't let it get in my hair! Keep it away from me!" she yelled, throwing up her hands to protect her face.

A moment later, she regained her composure. She crossed her arms tightly across her chest and clutched the collar of her blouse, pulling it up around her neck as if to protect herself from future butterfly attacks.

"Oh, I don't like things that fly," she said to Newton. "I don't like them at all. Do you know what my philosophy of life is? It's this: If it flies, kill it!"

Vanessa appeared in the doorway behind Mrs. Harbinger.

"There was no one there," Vanessa told Newton. "I didn't find Ruth Ann."

"Then what did I see?" asked Newton.

"I have no idea what you thought you saw," cut

in Mrs. Harbinger, "but what I said earlier is true. Ruth Ann can't talk to you. The reason is because she isn't here. She just wasn't feeling like herself this morning, so we sent her out of town to a specialist for observation."

"But what exactly is wrong with her?" asked Vanessa.

"Let's just say there appears to be some kind of a bug going around," said Mrs. Harbinger. "She'll be home in a couple of days. Why don't you try calling her then?"

Mrs. Harbinger pushed them both out of the doorway and started to close the front door.

"Wait, Mrs. Harbinger! Just one last question," called Vanessa. "What does, 'It's happening again,' mean?"

Mrs. Harbinger held the door open a crack and looked at Vanessa.

"What in heavens do you mean?"

"'It's happening again.' You said it yourself. I heard it on our answering machine."

"But that's not what I said at all," Mrs. Harbinger replied. "I didn't say, 'It's happening again.' I said, 'Happy Birthday, Ruth Ann.'"

Once again, she shut the door in their faces.

5.

A TOWN FULL OF SECRETS

Newton and Vanessa walked down Ruth Ann's long driveway and turned left when they reached the street.

Newton stayed on the sidewalk, but Vanessa hopped up onto a white picket fence that bordered the sidewalk and seemed to stretch into the distance for miles.

"What are you doing?" asked Newton.

"Fence walking," said Vanessa. "I've been doing this since I was a little kid. I hate being stuck on the ground. If I had my way, I'd repeal the law of gravity."

The top of the fence was thin, and each picket post had a blunt point on it, but somehow Vanessa was able to walk along the top of it, keeping perfect balance. "Ruth Ann was there," said Vanessa as they walked along. "I just know it."

"But her mother said she was gone," said Newton.

"Her mother's hiding something, I'm sure," said Vanessa. "Parents can be so strange. They never tell you anything. Everything always has to be such a big secret. And it's not just Ruth Ann's mother. Sometimes I get the feeling that everyone in this town is hiding something. It's a town full of secrets."

"I don't understand," said Newton. "What kind of secrets?"

"If I knew, then they wouldn't be secrets," said Vanessa. "It's just that whenever you ask people a question about the town, no one ever gives you an answer. Take something simple like — Why do the butterflies come to Angel Falls?"

"I don't know," said Newton.

"Neither does anybody else. At least, that's what they say. Or look at the name of this town, for instance. Angel Falls. There isn't a lake or a river within a hundred miles of here, let alone a waterfall. Why is it called Angel Falls? Where are the falls?" asked Vanessa. "Or better yet . . . where are the angels?"

They walked along in silence for a while.

"I don't know, Vanessa," said Newton finally. "You say that Ruth Ann's dramatic. I think maybe it's you who's the dramatic one. Whatever happened between you and Ruth Ann, anyway? You said you used to be best friends."

"We were," said Vanessa. "But she changed. I've been planning a special expedition all year long, and Ruth Ann was going to come with me, but suddenly she got a whole new group of friends, and she wanted to bring them, too. I said 'No,' and we had a fight, and we haven't been friends since then.

"Last week in school she saw me reading an old children's book I happened to have with me. She said people who are turning twelve shouldn't be reading baby books, and she told me to hide it before someone saw it and started telling people I looked like a baby. The old Ruth Ann would never have talked to me like that. Besides, I don't care if people think I look like a baby. I'm not interested in the way people look. I'm interested in the things people do."

They walked along, silent once more.

Newton watched Vanessa balancing her way along the thin edge of the top of the fence. The angled rays of the afternoon sun hit the fence full on, making the side that faced the sidewalk glow a bright white and leaving the side under the trees in shadow.

The sun kept getting in Newton's eyes, and he had to squint a little. One moment Vanessa would lean a little into the sun and he would think she looked young for her age — almost like a little girl up on the fence. The next minute she would lean a little into the shadow and he would lose sight of her, but mostly she looked strong and in control, and he thought he saw the hint of a smile on her lips that seemed to say, "I can do this. I've always been able to do this, and I always will." She made it look easy.

Finally, the fence ended, and Vanessa jumped down. She pointed down a side street.

"I turn here," she said. "Listen, you know that expedition I said I was planning. It has to do with the Emerald Rainbow butterflies. If you really want to see the butterfly migration, meet me at the field tomorrow morning at eight o'clock. You've got to be on time. If you're not, I'll just have to start without you." She waved good-bye, and in a moment she had vanished around the corner.

Later that night, as Newton turned out the light to go to sleep, he looked at the alarm clock. If there was one thing he liked, it was sleeping late on vacation mornings.

He set the alarm for 7:00 A.M.

6.

A BLiZZARD OF BUTTERFLiES

"**H**ere they come!" yelled Vanessa.

Newton tilted back his head and looked up in the direction Vanessa was pointing.

It was true. It was the next morning, and the butterflies had begun to arrive. The butterfly migration had reached Angel Falls.

Up over the treetops that edged the field came a line of butterflies. It was almost as if they were flying in formation, the way birds do.

The sun, which was already partway up the sky, hit their wings like a golden spotlight. Each time the wings opened and closed, they threw off a burst of rainbow colors.

The first line of butterflies passed overhead and disappeared above the treetops on the other side of the field. It was followed by another line and another line and another line — each line in perfect formation, each flying in the same direction.

After a while, the lines began to combine into wide bands of butterflies. Then finally these bands blended together until the sky above the field was one solid mass of butterflies, all flying at treetop height, all flying in one direction over the field.

"Why do they fly together like that?" Newton asked Vanessa.

"There are a lot of things about butterflies that no one really understands, and this is one of them," she replied. "You've probably seen flocks of birds migrating. Well, it turns out that some types of butterflies do the same thing. Some species migrate thousands of miles to the same places year after year. And no one knows why. The most famous are the Monarch butterflies."

Newton stood and watched the butterflies. If there were an eighth wonder of the world, Newton knew this would be it.

"Take this compass," said Vanessa, reaching into her backpack. "We have to keep an eye on which way they're moving."

Newton steadied the compass needle until it had stopped swinging and was pointing in one direction. Then he oriented the compass card until the "N" was under the point of the needle. He compared the direction the butterflies were flying with the compass.

"Northwest," he called. "They're flying northwest. What makes them all fly in one direction?"

"No one knows," said Vanessa. "Some scientists think they sense direction by using polarized light. Other scientists think they can sense changes in the earth's magnetic field. I was sure they would head for the sun. Sort of the way moths fly toward a light. But they're flying the other way."

"I think they're flying with the wind," said Newton.

Vanessa put her index finger into her mouth and licked it. Then she held it up into the air. The side that felt cooler would tell her which direction the wind was coming from.

"That's an interesting theory," she said. "It's true at the moment. We'll see what happens."

Newton looked up. Even though it was morning, the sky had become a little darker. He saw that there were now so many butterflies overhead they had partially blocked the light.

The wind began to die down a little and now some of the butterflies began to fly lower, drifting down from the sky and sweeping over the grass in the field. Newton could hear them now, too. They made a sort of soft rustling sound as their wings beat against the air.

Now, it wasn't just the sky, but the whole field from treetop level to the ground that was full of butterflies.

"How many do you think there are?" asked Vanessa.

Newton looked around. He started to calculate. If the field were such a distance long by such a distance wide, and the trees were such a distance tall, and there were a certain number of butter-flies per cubic meter. . . .

He swept out his arms. If the butterflies hadn't been so fast, he could have touched thirty in just one wave of his hand. How could he compute how many there were when the air was so full of butterflies that he was almost afraid to take a deep breath for fear of breathing them in?

"I don't know," he finally answered. "A thousand times a thousand would be way too few. Millions maybe, and they keep on coming."

"Miles!" shouted Vanessa. "Miles and miles of butterflies!"

"A blizzard!" yelled Newton. "A blizzard of butterflies!"

"Here's a very old riddle," Vanessa called out. "It runs through the valleys clapping its hands. What is it?"

Newton paused to think, but before he could answer, Vanessa said, "A butterfly, of course. Come on, let's run." And off she went, her arms flung wide.

Newton just stood there, feeling kind of foolish.

"Come on!" yelled Vanessa. "Don't be a stick-in-the-mud. It'll be good for you. It almost feels like flying." And then she was off again across the field, swooping and whirling, running with the butterflies.

Newton stuffed the compass in his pocket, grabbed Vanessa's pack, and slung it onto his back. Hesitantly, he raised both arms, looking over his shoulder to check that no one was watching what he was about to do. Then he began to run — slowly at first, but gradually picking up speed — into the gliding, swirling, flashing mass of butterflies.

"This is kind of fun," he thought.

And then he ran even faster to catch up with Vanessa.

7.
INTO THE WOODS

Vanessa was waiting for him on the far side of the field. "This way," she said. "Come on."

There was a little opening in the wall of woods at the edge of the field. Vanessa turned and walked quickly into this opening.

Newton followed and found that they were on a fairly wide path that led into the woods. He stopped and checked the compass, and then looked down the path. It headed approximately northwest. He looked up through the new leaves on the trees. Yes, he could just make out the butterflies, still flying overhead in the same direction.

There was no wind now, and he realized that his theory about butterflies flying with the wind was probably wrong. He wondered what made them all fly together. Was it just the habit of following the group, or some individual inner sense of direction that just happened to send them all off at once in the same direction?

They walked in silence through the woods, pausing now and then to check the compass. The path led down a hill and up another one. It twisted and turned a little, but still it kept leading them in the same general direction the butterflies were flying.

The sun filtered down through the trees, and although it was cool in the shade, the day soon became warm enough for Newton to remove his jacket and tie it around his waist.

They walked for a long time. Every now and then, Vanessa would run on ahead, then call back impatiently, "Come on," or "Let's go." To Newton, who was carrying her heavy backpack, it soon began to feel as if they'd been walking for twelve hours, although it might have been only twelve minutes.

"Are we there, yet?" he asked Vanessa after a while, making his voice sound like a little kid's.

"You can turn back any time you like," she replied. "But I intend to keep on until I find out where the butterflies are going, or until I fall off the edge of the earth, whichever comes first."

"What makes you think they're going anyplace at all?" asked Newton. "Maybe they're just passing through on their way to someplace else."

"I don't think so," said Vanessa. "They always arrive on almost the exact same day every year. Then they're everywhere for about a week. After that most of them do move on, but I think there's something special about Angel Falls that draws them here each year."

"Like what?" asked Newton.

"There are a couple of possibilities," said Vanessa. "Butterflies are very fussy about the food their babies can eat. There are more than twenty thousand types of butterflies and each type lays its eggs on a different type of plant so its baby caterpillars will be near the right kind of food the minute they hatch out of their eggs. If the caterpillar doesn't get the right food, it starves to death and never moves on to the next stage of its life to become a butterfly. So one possibility would be that there's an abundance of caterpillar food in Angel Falls.

"But I think it's more likely that there might be something here that attracts the adult butterflies. Adult butterflies usually don't eat much, but there might be a certain kind of wildflower that has a nectar they like to drink. Or maybe there's a special type of tree in Angel Falls that the adult butterflies like to rest on. Monarch butterflies fly thousands of miles each year to reach fir groves in Mexico or eucalyptus trees in Pacific Grove, California.

"I even read about one kind of butterfly that's been returning to a single silver beech tree in Iowa for over fifty years. And no one knows why or how different generations of that butterfly can find the same tree year after year. The thing is, people have been studying butterflies for years, but there's still a lot that needs to be learned about them."

"And what makes you so interested in butterflies?" asked Newton.

"How can you live in this town and not be interested in butterflies?" said Vanessa. "Besides, it's like a mystery. Didn't you ever want to find out about something simply because no one else knew the answer?"

Vanessa stopped short, and Newton thought

she was going to start to lecture him about something else. Then he looked up.

Just ahead, the path ended in a T-shaped intersection. A new path lay across theirs, so that they could turn sharply to the left or sharply to the right, but there was no way they could continue straight ahead.

Newton glanced at the compass and then looked up into the leaves. The butterflies were still flying northwest, which was straight ahead, but there was no path in that direction.

Vanessa looked down the path that led to her right. Then she looked to her left.

"Who needs a path," she said finally and plunged straight ahead into the underbrush in front of her, until she vanished from sight.

Newton heard her, thrashing through the undergrowth, blazing her own trail. Then there was silence.

"Are you coming or not?" called Vanessa. The thrashing resumed. "And don't forget the compass!" she yelled. "We're really going to need it now."

Newton took a deep breath and dove into the woods. Earlier, the way ahead had been fairly clear, and they had walked under the shelter of the tall trees of a mature forest. But now, things had changed, and they found themselves walking through a dense twisted thicket of young saplings.

Newton had walked in the woods before, but he'd never gone off the path. This was farther and deeper than he'd ever been, and he started to remember the warning the man in the black hat had given them the day before.

"You don't think we're getting lost, do you?" he asked.

"As long as we have the compass, we're fine," said Vanessa. "Besides, it's not as if Angel Falls is in the middle of a wilderness. We can't walk through the woods for that long without hitting something."

And that's exactly what happened a minute later.

Vanessa had pushed on ahead. Newton was still carrying her pack and wondering how she had managed to fit so many heavy, lumpy, unknown objects into such a small space, when he realized he no longer heard her thrashing through the trees ahead of him.

He trudged on up a small hill, and when he got to the top and looked down, he realized why he no longer heard Vanessa. The thicket had ended abruptly in a small clearing, and Vanessa had stopped.

Directly in front of her, blocking the path, was the tallest stone wall that Newton had ever seen.

8.
WHeRe THeRe'S A WALL, THeRe'S A WAY

Newton walked down the hill and stood next to Vanessa. Together, they gazed up at the wall.

It was built with huge blocks of gray stone that fit together almost seamlessly. Parts of the wall were covered with thin vines, but mostly it was just smooth stone. It looked very solid. Newton guessed that it was about eleven or twelve feet tall.

"I want to know what this wall is doing in the middle of the woods," said Vanessa. "I want to know why it's blocking my way. I want to know what's on the other side. And I want to know now!"

"What if we just stopped for a moment and looked around a little. . . ?" Newton started to say, but Vanessa was already trying to climb the wall.

"There aren't many handholds," she said.

She grabbed one of the vines, but it broke off instantly in her hands.

She turned to Newton. "Let me try to get up on your shoulders."

Newton stepped back.

"Are you sure we should be doing this?" he asked. "I mean, someone probably put that wall here for a reason."

Vanessa stopped.

"Do you think there's something behind there that someone's afraid will get out?" she asked.

"No," said Newton. "I think someone doesn't want us to get in."

"Where's your sense of adventure?" said Vanessa. "Where there's a wall, there's a way. Maybe I could dig my way under. Or maybe I could climb a tree and . . . oh, I wish it weren't so tall."

Newton had moved a little way off. He was now sitting down with his back against a vine-covered part of the wall, resting and watching Vanessa.

Something was cutting into his back, however . . . something underneath the vines. He turned and stared at the wall for a long minute.

Vanessa was still talking.

"Maybe if I walked all along the wall, I'd find a section where the stones had fallen," she was saying.

"Maybe," said Newton, "we should try the door."

"What door?"

"The one I'm leaning against," he said.

Vanessa rushed over, and Newton stood up. Together they pushed back the vines and looked at the door in the wall.

It was tall and wide, and appeared to be made out of a single piece of wood the same gray color as the wall.

The curious thing about it was that the entire surface was carved. As they looked closer, they could see that the door was covered with figures of all kinds of animals. There were familiar animals — a buffalo, a tiger, and a lion — but there were also animals that they didn't recognize, including a strange-looking bird that looked a little like a fat duck with a curved beak.

"I'm not a hundred percent sure," said Vanessa,

"but I think all these animals may be endangered or extinct."

Across the top of the door in raised capital letters were the words: HESPERIDES GARDEN.

The door had no doorknob or handle, no key or keyhole, no knocker or bell, and no visible hinges. It was just a door, sitting in a wall, with no apparent way of opening it.

"Let's try pushing it," said Vanessa.

They leaned against the door with all their weight, but it wouldn't budge. Sliding it sideways didn't work, either.

"You discovered it," said Vanessa. "Can't you think of some way to open it?"

"Well, in movies there's always a hidden latch or secret button," said Newton. "Maybe if we look closely, we'll spot something."

They tried spinning the head of a carved owl, but the owl was exactly what it seemed to be, an owl, nothing more, nothing less.

"I don't know about you, but I don't think this is going to work," said Vanessa. "What I do know is that I'd love to take home this butterfly. It looks just like a Xerces Blue. They used to be really common, but people built houses all over the places they lived, and now they're extinct."

She reached out and touched the left wing of the carved wooden butterfly, and it broke off, though she had barely touched it.

Vanessa jumped back in surprise, and that was when they saw that the wing wasn't broken at all. It had simply folded down, revealing an opening in the door. Vanessa pushed her hand inside.

"I think it's . . . Yes! It's a door handle!" she cried. "There *is* a secret latch, and I found it!"

She pushed down on the handle, and the door swung open easily on silent, hidden hinges. Newton grabbed Vanessa's backpack and together they stepped through.

9.

THE GARDEN

The world on the far side of the wall was very different from the close and crowded woods they had just come through.

"What is this place?" asked Vanessa when they stood on the other side of the door.

In front of them stretched a wide green lawn. All around the edges of the lawn, and leading off at angles into the distance, were rows of hedges about shoulder height. At the base of each hedge was a flower bed, each one different from the next. Some of the flowers were already in bloom.

In front of each flower bed was a thin row of very low shrubs, providing a protective front border to the flowers.

Here and there around the lawn were wooden benches. Tall shade trees sheltered the benches from the sun. It was indeed a garden, as the sign on the door had said, a garden that appeared to be well-kept and well-tended.

"Where are we?" asked Newton.

"I don't know," answered Vanessa. "I've lived in Angel Falls all my life, and I've never heard of any place like this."

"Who made it? Who takes care of it?" asked Newton.

"I just told you I don't know," said Vanessa. "But there's something about it that seems familiar."

"Look at this," said Newton.

A few steps from where they were standing was a wooden post with a sign attached at the top. Carved into the sign were the following words:

WELCOME TO HESPERIDES GARDEN.

TAKE ONLY PICTURES.

LEAVE ONLY FOOTPRINTS.

A little farther on was another sign. This one read:

MORE IS HIDDEN THAN VISIBLE.

BE AWARE AS YOU PROCEED.

At the base of this sign was the beginning of a path.

"Shall we 'follow the yellow brick road'?" asked Newton. He pointed to the path.

But Vanessa had stopped. She craned her head and looked up. Newton followed her gaze.

Directly overhead were the butterflies. Rows and rows of them, still flying toward their unknown destination. But now they seemed to be much lower. A few of them sailed low over the wall and skimmed the grass not far from Newton, but most of them continued on and disappeared over a row of trees on the far edge of the lawn.

"This could be it," whispered Vanessa.

She looked at Newton for a moment. Then, together, they started down the path. As they passed some of the flower beds, they saw that each one was labeled with a little sign pushed into the soil, telling what type of flower bloomed there.

Vanessa kept running on ahead. She was watching the butterflies above her, but she kept pausing at one flower bed after the other, reading the signs. She had a puzzled look on her face, as if she were trying to figure out a mystery that was just out of reach. Then, she stopped short, spun around, and raced back to Newton. The puzzled look had changed to a look of excitement.

"I know why this place seems familiar!" she cried. "I've read about this, but I've never seen one, that's why I couldn't figure it out. It's a butterfly garden!

"Each of these flowers attracts a specific kind of butterfly. The milkweed attracts Monarch butterflies, of course. It's the plant they lay their eggs on. Everyone knows that. The nettles attract Red Admiral butterflies. And look, lilacs. Tiger Swallowtails love lilacs. I've never heard of a butterfly garden that was as large as this one is, though."

Vanessa hurried them along the path and through the line of trees. They were still in the garden, and now they both saw something that made them stop short.

"Oh!" The same word came out of both their mouths at once.

In front of them was an open area, with no flowers or hedges. And in the middle of the open space was a tree. It was very tall, and it had many leafy branches covered with white blossoms.

Newton stood and stared at the tree. There was something about it, something that made it seem to be almost a living creature. It almost looked to Newton as if the tree were breathing, and then he realized what it was that gave it that appearance.

The tree was covered with butterflies. They crowded each branch and perched up and down the trunk. They rose and fell together in great clouds all around the top, and this, combined with the gentle sighing of their wings beating the air, was what gave the impression that the tree was breathing.

Vanessa ran to the tree and touched it, then she ran back to where Newton was standing and flopped down into the grass, her eyes on the tree.

"I found it!" she said. "Let's have lunch."

10.
UNDER THE TREE

Newton could see that Vanessa was trying to act calm, but she kept bouncing up and down with excitement. She was behaving as if she had made a major scientific discovery, but she didn't seem ready to explain it to him, yet.

Instead she reached for her pack.

Now Newton finally found out what it was he had been carrying for so long. Vanessa opened her pack and pulled out a tablecloth, which she spread on the ground. Next came a hardcover book.

"What are you reading?" asked Newton.

"Oh nothing," said Vanessa quickly, turning the book face down. She placed it carefully on a corner of the tablecloth. Then she hesitated, reached back down, and turned the book right side up. It was *Peter Pan* by James M. Barrie.

"All right," she said. "If you must know, it's the book Ruth Ann told me to hide last week. It's part of my collection of children's books."

She reached into her pack and pulled out a thermos bottle of lemonade.

"I don't want to hear any comments from you about my collection," she continued. "It's very important to me and quite valuable. Let's talk about something else."

She reached into the bottomless pit of her pack one more time and pulled out a small white box.

"Today's my birthday," she said.

Inside the box was a tiny, perfect birthday cake. It was in surprisingly good shape considering how much jostling the backpack had received. The top was decorated with green candy leaves and butterflies. Across the middle in hard sugar letters was written:

HAPPY 12TH BIRTHDAY,

VANESSA A. ZEPHYR

"I know everyone thinks I'm the youngest one in our class, but I'm not," said Vanessa, pulling forks, knives, and napkins out of her pack. "It's just the way I seem, somehow."

"They won't think you're the youngest any-more," said Newton. "I won't be twelve until the end of the year."

"May I cut you a piece?" asked Vanessa. "It's homemade."

"Homemade?" said Newton. "It looks like it came from a bakery. You're lucky to have a mother who can make cakes like that."

"What makes you assume that only mothers make cakes?" asked Vanessa. "Actually . . . I baked it myself. My mother's dead," she added quietly.

"I'm so sorry," said Newton. "I didn't know."

Vanessa held up her hand. "It's okay," she said. "It happened a long time ago when I was a little girl. Our house turned into a bit of a disaster area for a while — my father got sort of withdrawn, and he hasn't really talked to me much since then — but I try to look on the bright side. We both come and go as we please. I could stay up all night if I wanted. And, I've learned to do a lot of things on my own. For instance, I make all my own meals, including birthday cakes. And now that I'm twelve, I'm practically grown up. I really don't need anybody's help with anything."

Newton didn't know what to say. He hadn't meant to pry into her personal life, especially if it brought up sad memories. He looked down at the cake. "What does the 'A' stand for?" he asked, trying to change the subject.

"Adventure," said Vanessa, perking up. "Adventure is my middle name."

"No," said Newton. "Really?"

"Well . . . maybe it is, and maybe it isn't. Maybe I have a middle name I don't really like. But if I could choose, I'd choose Adventure. What's your middle name?"

"I don't have one," said Newton. "My parents said when I got older I could pick my own middle name if I wanted to," he added.

"Then we'll have to think of one for you," said Vanessa. "Everyone should have a middle name that expresses their character."

She turned to the cake and cut them each a piece.

"I didn't know that today was your birthday," said Newton. "I would have gotten you a present. Maybe tomorrow . . ."

"It's not necessary," said Vanessa.

"Oh, but I want to," said Newton. "Everyone should get presents on their birthday. Is there anything you really want?"

"Why don't you surprise me. I like birthday surprises. But you really don't have to. I've already got the best present I could ever have. I've discovered why the butterflies come to Angel Falls. It's the tree. There's something about it that draws them here. And now maybe . . ."

Her voice trailed off.

"Now maybe what?" asked Newton.

Vanessa took a deep breath, and then her words came out all in a rush.

"Well . . . there is something else I've always wanted. You have to promise not to tell anyone about this, and you have to promise not to laugh. It's probably going to sound silly to you, but I think you might understand. Have you ever heard of the Butterfly Dream?"

Newton shook his head, no, and Vanessa continued.

"Over two thousand years ago there was a Chinese philosopher named Chuang Tsu who studied butterflies. And one night he dreamed that he *was* a butterfly. When he woke up, he thought about the dream and said, 'I do not know whether I was then a man dreaming I was a butterfly, or whether I am now a butterfly dreaming I am a man.' After he had the dream he was never sure.

"Whenever I study butterflies I think about that dream, and it reminds me of my own dream: Ever since I was a little girl, I've wanted to fly. That's been my dream . . . to really fly. When I was younger, I tried everything: jumping out of trees, making paper wings . . . everything. But nothing ever worked. I'd just about given up hope when I started studying the Emerald Rainbow butterflies. I discovered that they're a little bit different from other butterflies in the way their scales cover the surface of their wings. Their scales are attached very loosely, and they easily fall off and disintegrate into a fine green powder. I believe that if I can collect enough of that powder, I may be able to use it to fly. That's the real reason I've always wanted to find where the butterflies go. Okay, you can laugh now."

Newton didn't laugh, but he was skeptical to say the least.

"What are you going to do with this powder, eat it?" he asked.

"No, I believe that if I rub it on my arms I'll be able to fly."

"Sort of like in *Peter Pan*?"

"Now you are laughing at me," said Vanessa, and she began to pack up the lunch things in quick jerky movements.

"I'm not laughing," said Newton. "It just doesn't sound very scientific. You're going to rub green powder on your arms, and it will make you fly?"

"Yes, that's what I believe. If you must know, I've already tried it."

"And did it work?"

"How could it? I didn't have enough of the powder to make it work. But now — I've found the source."

She stood up and pulled a large jar out of the pack. Then she picked up a spoon and walked over to the tree. Newton followed.

The tree was very old. Its base was so wide around that it would have taken five or six people holding hands to encircle it. The lower trunk had no branches, but was full of deep creases and wrinkles. Even though the tree had obviously stood there a long time, it appeared to be healthy and strong.

The tree's blossoms gave off a pure, sweet, flowery scent, but there was another smell, too, just as pleasant but different.

"I think that's the butterflies," said Vanessa. "They've marked the tree with their scent. I think it helps them find it year after year, although no one is really sure if butterflies use their sense of smell to navigate."

All around the base of the tree was a fine green powder. There was powder, too, in the crooks and crevasses of the tree's limbs and bark. Vanessa scraped the powder carefully off the ground with the spoon, and then she began to climb the tree, scraping more powder off the tree itself. She moved slowly and cautiously, taking care not to injure any butterflies.

Newton stayed on the ground, watching. He walked around the tree several times, and after a while he began to notice things. The first thing was that one of the branches of the tree had no leaves and looked darker than the rest of it. The second thing he noticed was that all around the tree for a circle of thirty or forty feet, very little grew.

"The tree looks like it's been in a fire," he called to Vanessa, who had climbed up out of sight.

"That's very possible," she yelled. "It's the tallest thing around. It's probably been hit by lightning."

"What kind of tree is it?" he called.

"I don't know. I've never seen anything like it before," Vanessa answered.

Newton sat down and waited for Vanessa. After a while she climbed back down, being careful not to disturb any of the butterflies that clung to the tree. Keeping one hand behind her, she approached Newton, holding the jar in front of her with her other hand. The jar was filled with green powder.

"I don't know if this will do it," she said. "But it's certainly more than I've ever seen before in one place. I'm going to take it home and analyze it tonight. Then maybe, if you're not laughing too hard, I might allow you to watch me test it."

She set the jar down. Then she brought her other hand out from behind her back.

"Look at this," she said. "I picked it off the tree. It seems awfully early in the season for apples."

She held in her hand something that looked like a piece of fruit. It was shaped like an apple, but it was golden like an orange, and its skin was fuzzy, not smooth.

She held it out to Newton.

"It doesn't look like an apple to me," said Newton. "It looks more like a peach."

"I dare you to eat it," said Vanessa.

"Who are we supposed to be, Adam and Eve?" He looked at the piece of fruit in her hand. "There's no way I'm going to eat something we found growing wild in the woods," he said. "What if it's poisonous? Promise me you're not going to eat it, either."

Vanessa rolled her eyes.

"I promise you I'm not about to take a single bite," she said.

Suddenly her eyes lit up.

"I've got it," she said. "How about Adam?"

"What?" asked Newton.

"For a middle name for you. Adam, like in Adam and Eve."

Newton couldn't tell if she was laughing at him or not. He thought about it for a minute.

"Madam, I'm *not* Adam," he finally said. Then he added, "That's a famous palindrome: Madam, I'm Adam. It's spelled the same forward or backward."

"I know what a palindrome is," said Vanessa. "Last year at school . . ."

Just then they heard a rustling noise in some tall grass, far off to their left.

"Someone's coming," said Newton.

Vanessa quickly dropped the fruit, and the two

of them stood there and tried to see who was approaching. The rustling grew louder, and then they saw that the grass was bending and buckling as something moved through it in a wave-shaped motion.

"I think it's a snake," said Vanessa.

"Then it's going to be the biggest snake either of us has ever seen," said Newton.

They waited for the snake or whatever it was to appear, but the movement stopped, and nothing emerged from the tall grass.

"Maybe it's watching us," said Vanessa.

"Let's get out of here," said Newton.

They threw all their stuff into Vanessa's open backpack. Newton grabbed it, and they raced back to the door in the wall. It was still open, just as they'd left it. Vanessa stepped through, and as Newton pulled the door shut behind them, he noticed that a sign was carved on the inside of the door. It said:

LIFE IS A GARDEN.

EVERYTHING THAT GROWS MUST CHANGE.

11.

THE SWING

The next morning, Newton stood in front of Vanessa's house, wondering if it was too early to ring the front doorbell. They had agreed to meet at the apple tree in the field, and Newton had gotten up early again (two days in a row on a vacation was a record for him), but Vanessa had never come.

He hadn't known exactly where she lived, but he had gone back and followed the side street she'd walked down two days ago when they'd first met. Sure enough, he had found her driveway, marked by a big mailbox labeled, "Zephyr."

In one hand, Newton held a wrapped birthday present. With the other hand, he reached up and pushed the button by the side of the door. Inside the house he could faintly hear a buzzer announce his presence up and down the halls. He waited to hear footsteps coming to answer the doorbell, but no one came.

He stepped back and looked at the house. All the shades were drawn on both the first and second floors. It had the look of a house where no one was home.

Newton decided to walk around to the back. Perhaps Vanessa was in the backyard and hadn't heard him. As he started down the gravel walk along the side of the house, he heard a strange sound. It was a metallic screeching that repeated over and over at regular intervals.

Cautiously, Newton rounded the corner and stepped into the backyard.

There was a stone terrace along the rear of the house that looked out on a wide expanse of unmowed lawn. Just at the edge, where the terrace met the grass, stood an old swing set.

A man was sitting on one of the swings, facing out over the lawn, and swinging back and forth. He seemed lost in thought. Each time the swing got to the top of its backward arc, the man gave a slow, halfhearted kick. As the swing lurched forward, it made a protesting screech.

The man didn't see Newton at first, but as Newton came to a stop by the corner of the house, the man looked up. An expression of surprise passed quickly over his face and then was gone.

It was a man Newton had seen before — a man wearing a black baseball hat and mirrored glasses. Newton wondered what he was doing in Vanessa's backyard.

"So, we meet again," called the man, letting the swing rock to a stop. "It's been a long time since I've been on one of these," he added, patting the swing seat. "I'd forgotten how close this comes to knowing what *they* must feel." He pointed straight up at a band of Emerald Rainbow butterflies flying just above treetop level.

Newton watched the butterflies for a moment. Then he looked back at the empty butterfly net the man held across his knees.

The man saw where Newton was looking. "I always carry it with me," he said. "I'm a lepidopterist."

Newton had no idea what that meant. It

sounded like the name of a rare disease. Or was it something to do with leopards?

"Lepidopterists study butterflies," continued the man. "I'm waiting to talk with Vanessa about some of her research on the local species, but she's late. I thought I saw her in those woods northwest of town yesterday, after I'd warned you both not to go there. You haven't been in those woods with her, have you?"

Despite the man's seemingly friendly manner, Newton could feel the eyes behind the mirrored glasses studying him. He stayed rooted to his spot near the corner of the house and tried to change the subject.

"So, uh . . . how do you know Vanessa?" Newton asked.

"She didn't tell you?" asked the man. He hesitated for a moment, then he leaned back in the swing and began swinging. "Vanessa and I go way back. I've known her since she was a baby. Tell me again, what did you say your name was?"

"It's Newton," said Newton.

"Newton? Ah! After Sir Isaac Newton, no doubt. A good scientific name. A practical name with a touch of gravity to it. Newton, why don't you come over here and join me?" said the man, indicating the swing next to his. "I assume you're waiting for Vanessa, too. We can wait for her together."

Newton walked reluctantly over to the swing set and sat down. He held Vanessa's birthday present on his lap.

The man looked at him as his swing passed by. "Names are very important, don't you think?" asked the man. "Did Vanessa tell you how she got her name? No? Her parents were lepidopterists, too. They named her after a butterfly they were studying. Its common name is the Red Admiral, but its scientific name in Latin is Vanessa atalanta. Vanessa, in fact, is the name of a whole group of butterflies. And Atalanta was the name of a young woman in Greek legend who could run faster than anyone. The only time she lost a race was when she stopped in the middle to pick up a golden apple. Vanessa Atalanta. I've always thought it was a beautiful name."

As the man talked, Newton leaned back and began to swing, too, but he was thinking that now he knew something about Vanessa that she didn't realize he knew. Now he knew her real middle name.

"Names are funny things," continued the man with the black hat. "Did you know that the name Psyche means both butterfly and soul in Greek? Up until the early 1900s many people believed that moths and butterflies were really the souls of the dead. You should hear some of the names scholars gave to moths: the Mourning Underwing, for example."

The man pumped his swing higher and tried to match the arc of its movement with Newton's, but Newton remembered that Vanessa had warned him about talking to this man, so whenever the man swung faster, Newton slowed down.

"So, Newton," said the man. "Tell me about yourself. Tell me your hopes, your fears, your dreams. Perhaps you intend to be a lepidopterist, too?"

"I'm only eleven," said Newton. He was not used to being up in the air this much, and he was getting a little dizzy.

"Ah, I see you're a hard man to pin down. But a person must have a dream in life — perhaps many dreams."

The man stared into the distance. His swing began to lose momentum. He appeared to Newton to have momentarily forgotten what he was talking about, or where he was.

Suddenly the man snapped back to attention.

"I've been on this swing too long," he said, dragging his feet until he stopped. His voice turned serious. "There's something about Vanessa that you should know. She has a very vivid imagination. Ever since her mother died, I've often wondered if she knows when something is real and when it isn't. For instance, there's this flying nonsense. Don't pretend to look so surprised. I know all about it, and I have to tell you, it worries me. It deeply worries me, more than you could ever know."

The man lowered his voice almost to a whisper.

"I don't like things that fly," he said. "I used to, but not anymore. I study them, but I don't like them."

He stood up. "I'm afraid I'll have to leave without seeing Vanessa," he said. "I'm on the trail of something big. But I'd like to have a little agreement with you, Newton. I'd like you to keep your eyes open. If you, or Vanessa, or any of your friends should see anything . . . anything new or different, like a new species of butterfly for instance, I'd like you to let me know. I might be able to help you identify it."

The man touched his hat in a sort of good-bye salute. "If you see Vanessa," he said, "tell her I was here." Then he walked slowly away, disappearing behind the corner of the house.

12.

DON'T GO UPSTAIRS

After the man left, Newton went back to the front porch. Where was Vanessa?

Newton wondered if he should just turn around and walk back home. Maybe Vanessa didn't want to see him. And yet, she had said she would meet him. He still didn't know her very well, but he had a feeling that when Vanessa said she was going to do something, she did it . . . unless an emergency got in her way.

He tried to think what Vanessa would do if she were in his place, and he knew the answer. He walked up to the front door, turned the knob, and pushed the door open.

"Hello," he called. "Is anybody home?"

He stood still and listened. Any moment now, he thought, Vanessa or perhaps her father would call out a greeting, but there was no answer.

Newton walked into the front hallway. It was cool inside the house, cool and dim. It took a moment for his eyes to get used to the light. In front of him a passage led back into the first floor of the house. To his right, a wide sweeping staircase led upstairs.

Newton listened again for the sound of someone in the house, but all he could hear was silence. Silence and the steady ticking of a tall old grandfather clock that stood just inside the front door.

He decided that Vanessa's room was most likely to be on the second floor, so he started up the stairs. "It's quiet," he thought. "Too quiet. Why do I feel like the kid in every horror movie who insists on going upstairs when everyone in the audience is yelling, 'No, no, don't go upstairs!'"

The third step creaked when he stepped on it, and he nearly jumped, but he kept on climbing until he reached the top.

The stairs ended in a long hallway with a number of doors leading off it. Newton began to walk down the hall. He had no idea how he would find Vanessa's room, until he came to a door with a huge sign on it. The sign read in giant letters: NO TRESPASSING!! Across the bottom of the sign someone had written in smaller letters: UNLESS IT'S YOU.

Newton knocked on the door.

The door was not shut all the way, and it swung open under the force of his knock. Any doubts he might have had that this was Vanessa's room vanished as he stepped inside.

At first glance the room looked like the ordinary bedroom of a twelve-year-old girl who is lucky enough to have her own room. There was a bed with a down comforter folded neatly across the bottom half. There was a chest of drawers with a small music system on top. There was a desk with a personal computer and printer. There was a night table with a telephone and a digital clock that appeared to be broken. It kept flashing, "12:00, 12:00, 12:00," over and over in bright green numbers.

But Newton knew it was Vanessa's room because of the ceiling and the walls. The ceiling was very high, and it had been painted a robin's egg blue with white fluffy clouds here and there.

The walls were covered with posters. The posters were not portraits of singers or musicians or movie stars. They were all images of flight. There were posters of butterflies, posters of people hang-gliding, a poster of a ballet called *The Firebird,* even a poster of the earth from space.

Against one wall, next to the desk, were several bookcases filled with books. One tall bookcase was different from the others. It was fitted with glass doors and locks. Newton glanced inside at some of the titles on the books' spines: *The Summer Birds* by Penelope Farmer, *Five Children and It* by E. Nesbit, *The Fledgling* by Jane Langton, *Green Mansions* by W. H. Hudson. There were lots more. This had to be Vanessa's book collection. He didn't recognize even a quarter of the books, but most of them appeared to be children's books, and he was pretty sure from reading the titles and looking at the few front covers that were visible that they all had something to do with flying.

Next to the bookshelf, pinned to the wall above the desk with a green pushpin was a piece of drawing paper. The paper had once been white, but now it was yellowed. It was a crayon drawing of what Newton supposed was a woman.

The drawing was little more than a stick figure standing under a tent of yellow squiggly lines that Newton realized must be hair. Pieces of white cotton that looked something like clouds had been glued to the paper just below her feet, and as Newton looked closer, he saw that what he had at first thought was an extra pair of arms looked on second glance like a set of wings.

At the bottom someone had written in block letters, MOTHER/ANGEL BY VANESSA, AGE 3.

Next to the drawing, under glass in a small black frame, was a clipping out of an old newspaper: a faded photograph of a woman below the headline, LOCAL SCIENTIST DIES IN FIRE.

Newton turned and looked around the rest of the room. It was definitely Vanessa's room all right, but where was Vanessa?

The morning sun streamed in from a window by Vanessa's bed, and a ray of light illuminated a spot on her desk. In the middle of that spot sat the jar of green powder that Vanessa had collected the day before. Yesterday, the jar had been full. Now half the powder was gone. As Newton stared at the jar, he thought the green powder almost looked as if it was glowing.

He looked back at the window. It was wide open and a breeze was blowing the curtains back against the bed.

What if Vanessa had tried the powder, Newton wondered. What if she had tried the powder and then opened the window and. . . .

He rushed toward the window, but he never got there, because as he came around the corner of the bed there was a sound from somewhere behind him in the room.

Newton stopped short and slowly turned. There was no one there, but as he stood still and listened, he thought he heard a noise from inside the closet.

Newton tiptoed up to the closet door and leaned forward.

"Is anybody in there?" he whispered.

And it was exactly at that moment that the closet door crashed open, and a claw thrust itself forward toward his face.

Newton had never run so fast in his life.

13.
THE THING

Newton was out the door, through the hall, and halfway down the staircase when something inside him made him stop.

He sat down on the stairs to think. If there was a creature in Vanessa's room, then Vanessa was in trouble. And if somehow the creature was, or had once been, Vanessa, then she was in even worse trouble.

He sat there on the step, half of him wanting desperately to run down the stairs and out the front door, and the other half of him wondering if he was brave enough to go back and help Vanessa.

Finally, he stood, and tiptoed back up the stairs and down the hall to Vanessa's room. He felt it was probably the bravest thing he had ever done in his life. He also had a feeling it might be the last thing he ever did in his life.

Vanessa's door was closed, and when he turned the doorknob, he found it was locked. He knocked on the door and listened. Inside the room he heard paper rustling and then the sound of something scurrying across the floor.

"Vanessa, are you in there?" he called.

Something came sliding under the door.

Newton jumped back, then looked down. It was a piece of lined notebook paper with a note written on it in strange scratchy handwriting. He reached down and picked it up.

"Go away!!!" it said.

"Vanessa, it's Newton," he called. "Are you all right?"

A moment later, another piece of paper came slipping under the door.

"No, I'm not all right. Leave me alone!"

Newton knocked again on the door.

"I brought you a birthday present," he said. "And I'm not leaving until I give it to you and see that you're okay."

Another moment went by. Then he heard the sound of a click as the door was unlocked, followed by the strange scurrying sound again.

Newton opened the door and stood in the doorway, looking into the room.

At first it seemed as if no one was there, and yet Newton knew someone, or something, was waiting for him. He was about to go look under the bed, when he heard a new sound. It was a sort of unhappy sigh, and it came from behind the open bedroom door. Newton walked into the room, turned, and slowly swung the door shut.

The sight that met his eyes was like nothing he had ever seen in his life. There, staring back at him from behind the door, was a *thing*.

It was bright green. On each side of its head were six small eyes, and it had incredibly large jaws. There were three pairs of short jointed arms with claws near the top of its body, and five pairs of shorter, stubby legs lower down. It was using the bottommost pair of legs to balance itself upright, so that it seemed just about as tall as Newton. It was fuzzy or furry, he couldn't tell which. All in all, it looked like a cross between a big green bear and some kind of an insect.

For a moment Newton and the thing gazed at each other face to face. The next instant, the thing jumped to the floor, and with a speed that amazed Newton, scuttled across the room into the closet, slamming the door behind it.

"Who are you?" called Newton.

A note shot out from under the door.

"I knew who I was when I went to bed last night, but I seem to have changed since then. Is this my birthday surprise?"

Newton walked closer and leaned against the closet door.

"Vanessa?" he asked through the door. "Is it you?"

Another note appeared at his feet. He picked it up.

"Is this what it's like to be twelve? I thought it would be different. Yesterday, when I looked at myself in the mirror, I saw . . . me. Today, I don't even recognize myself."

Newton let the note drop back to the floor.

"Vanessa, won't you talk to me at least?" he asked.

Another note appeared.

"I've tried, but on top of everything else, I seem to have lost my voice. At least I can still write . . . and think. I feel like I'm still me on the inside. At least I think so."

A thought crossed Newton's mind as he read the note. His voice turned cold.

"Wait a minute. How do I know you really are Vanessa? Maybe you're some alien pod creature from outer space who's taken over Vanessa's body. Well, not her body, I guess, but maybe you've stolen her brain."

The next note came sailing out so fast and furiously that Newton had to run across the room to retrieve it.

"G.M.A.B." was all it said.

A moment later another note emerged.

"I learned that from Ruth Ann. It means Give Me A Break."

"I wish you'd give me a break, Vanessa," Newton said. "I don't understand what's happened to you."

"Oh, I know exactly what's happened to me," said Vanessa's next note. "I'm a . . . thing."

"But what kind of a thing?" asked Newton. "I saw a movie once in which a guy woke up one morning and found he'd turned into a giant cockroach. Is that what's happened to you? Do you think maybe you're a giant cockroach?"

"Newton, where have you lived all your life?" said the next note. "It's obvious what's happened to me. All I wanted to do was fly like a butterfly, but instead I'm stuck crawling with my nose to the ground. This is not what I'd planned at all. I've turned into a caterpillar. A giant green Emerald Rainbow caterpillar!"

The closet door slowly opened, and the thing that was Vanessa emerged. She stood there, balancing at full height on her lower stubby legs, and Newton saw that what she had said was true. She was indeed a caterpillar. A very very large caterpillar.

"Vanessa," Newton said. "Maybe we should get some help. What about your father? Maybe you should tell him."

The Vanessa-thing dropped to the floor, scurried across the room, and vanished under the bed.

A note soon appeared.

"How can I tell him? I can't talk. Anyway, I don't plan to let him know. He never talks to me. Why should I talk to him?"

"But won't he know just by looking at you?" asked Newton.

"We live on such different schedules, we hardly ever see each other," said the next note. "Besides, he's so preoccupied with his work, I don't think he'd notice even if I were standing right in front of him. No, I don't want any help. I'm just going to wait and see what happens. Now, let's talk about something else. Something more fun. Where's my birthday present?"

"Uhh . . . I don't think it's something you'll like, Vanessa," said Newton. "Let me get you something else."

A short, jointed arm popped out from under the bed. Its claws opened and closed.

"Okay," said Newton. "Here you go."

He placed the present into the outstretched claw. The arm popped back under the bed.

Newton could hear the sound of wrapping paper being torn away. There was silence for a moment, then the sound of writing, and then the arm reappeared, holding the present.

Newton's gift had been a book. Now, he carefully took it back from the claw, along with a new note.

"*Magnificent Monsters from the Movies*. Thank you. I'm sure it's a favorite of yours, but I'm not in the mood to look at it right now. Could you put it on my desk, please?"

Newton could hear the unhappy sighing sound again. After a while it stopped, and a new note appeared.

"What did I do to deserve this? All I wanted to do was fly. Is that too much to ask for? What if I'm stuck like this forever — trapped inside the body of a giant green caterpillar?"

Newton didn't have an answer. He tried to think of something to say that might cheer her up.

"Did you hear about the two caterpillars that were walking across the top of a cereal box?" he asked. "The first caterpillar suddenly started running really fast until she got to the other side. When the second one caught up with her, he asked, 'Why did you start running so fast?' And the first caterpillar replied, 'Didn't you see the sign? It said: Tear along the dotted line.'"

Another note slid out from under the bed.

"Newton, please, no caterpillar jokes. I don't feel so great. I feel like I've lost all my energy. Do you think you could go to the kitchen and get me some food? And hurry, I feel like I could eat just about anything."

14.

WHAT DO CATERPILLARS EAT?

Newton raced into the hall, then leapt down the stairs two at a time. At the bottom, he turned and followed the passage that he'd seen when he'd first entered the house.

There were three doors at the end of the passage. They were all closed.

Newton tried the one in the middle first. Behind it was a broom closet. The door on the right did not lead to the kitchen, either. It opened onto a small bathroom. Finally, he tried the third door. This door did indeed open on the kitchen.

Vanessa had said she made all her own meals, and as Newton checked the refrigerator and looked in cabinets, he decided that she did all her own food shopping, too. Everywhere he turned were packages of store-bought snack foods and desserts.

He found a tray and loaded it up with as many different foods as he could find. Then he carried them all back up to Vanessa's room. He dumped everything out on Vanessa's desk, opened a bag of potato chips, placed it on the tray, and slid it under the bed.

There was a crunching sound, followed quickly by gagging and coughing. The bag and tray came flying out from under the bed, chips sailing across the room.

A note followed.

"They taste awful. They must be stale. What else have you got?"

Newton grabbed a Milky Way chocolate bar, a package of Hostess Twinkies, a bag of Pepperidge Farm Mint Milano cookies, and a handful of Hershey's Kisses. He put them all on the tray and pushed them under the bed.

A moment later everything came flying back

out again. Newton had to duck to avoid being hit by the tray.

There were twelve wet spots that looked like tears on the note that soon followed.

"I don't know what's wrong with me," the note said. "I'm starving, and these are all my favorite foods, but I just can't eat any of them."

"Don't worry," Newton called out, "I've got a whole ton of stuff here. Maybe you need some protein. That always works when I'm hungry."

As quickly as he could, he slapped together a peanut butter sandwich. It was rejected almost immediately. The sandwich came flying across the room and plopped onto the floor. It was not a pretty sight.

Newton sighed.

"Vanessa," he said. "There's a scene in the movie *Little Shop of Horrors* where the hero is talking to this man-eating plant. He asks it if it wants water, and it says no. He asks it if it wants more soil, and it says no. Finally, he gets fed up and says, 'What do you want, blood?' And you know what the answer was. Do you think you're like that? You're not a people-eating caterpillar are you?"

Newton waited for a note in answer to his question, but no note appeared.

"Vanessa, are you still there?" he finally asked.

Newton heard the pen scratching slowly across paper, and then a note appeared.

"Very weak. Very hungry."

"Vanessa, I've got an idea," said Newton. "What do real caterpillars eat?"

The note was a long time coming.

"Every kind eats one specific thing. I told you that already."

"Well, you said you're a giant Emerald Rainbow caterpillar. What do they eat?" called Newton.

The sound of the pen was slower with each note.

"Don't know," came the reply. "No such thing as giant Emerald Rainbow caterpillar. Except for me."

"What about the little Emerald Rainbow caterpillars?" yelled Newton. "What do they eat?"

Newton heard the pen writing with agonizing slowness.

And then it stopped.

"Vanessa?" asked Newton. "Vanessa!"

He reached under the bed and dragged out the

last note. It read, "Yuck! Little Emerald Rainbow caterpillars eat —"

And that was all.

"Vanessa!" yelled Newton. "What do they eat? What do Emerald Rainbow caterpillars eat?"

But there was no reply.

"If I can just get her some food, I know she'll be all right," thought Newton. "I've got to find out what Emerald Rainbow caterpillars eat. But where?"

Just then he happened to look up at one of the posters on Vanessa's wall. He'd seen it before, but he hadn't looked at it carefully until now. It showed the outline of a person's head with books flying around inside like butterflies.

But it was the seven words at the bottom of the poster that made Newton jump up and head for the door. This is what the seven words said:

YOU CAN FIND IT AT THE LIBRARY.

15.
I NEVER MET-A-MORPHOSIS
I DIDN'T LIKE

The streets and sidewalks were packed with people when Newton rode his bicycle into the heart of town. All the stores he passed had "Butterfly Week Sidewalk Sales Days" signs in the windows, and racks of special items for sale out on the sidewalk. When Newton finally maneuvered and dodged his way to the library, he locked his bike in the bike rack and dashed up the front steps.

There was a wide open space just inside the door that led up to the checkout desk. There were several armchairs in this area, and people were sitting in them, reading. A few of the people looked up as Newton entered. He always felt as if he were walking onstage or into a movie when he walked into the library.

Newton had been in the library before, but he always went straight to the film and video section, which was on the third floor. He'd taken out a number of movies, but he couldn't remember the last time he'd checked out a book.

Newton looked around. He realized that he didn't know where to begin. Where were the books about caterpillars, anyway?

"May I help you?" asked a voice behind him.

"I'm looking for books about caterpillars," said Newton, turning. He was about to say more, but he stopped short.

Standing before him was the man in the black hat. The thought crossed Newton's mind that this man seemed to show up everywhere, sort of like the black monolith in *2001: A Space Odyssey.*

"You didn't seem very interested in caterpillars this morning," said the man. "What made you change? Hmmm?"

The man was still wearing his mirrored glasses even though he was indoors. Newton wondered why the man always wore those glasses. Was he shielding his eyes from something . . . or was there something so terrible about his eyes that he wore the glasses to protect anyone who looked at him?

Newton stared into the glasses. As hard as he tried to look through the mirrored surface, he could not see the man's eyes, but he got the feeling that the man saw everything.

Newton didn't know what to say. He couldn't tell the man about Vanessa, but he didn't want to lie, either.

"It's hard to explain," he finally blurted. Then he turned and walked away as quickly as he could.

Ahead of him he spotted the open door of the elevator to the upper floors of the library. He walked straight inside and pushed the first button he could find.

The elevator stopped on the second floor, and the door opened. Newton stepped out . . . and stopped.

In front of him was a crowd of small children. They were sitting on the floor, with their heads turned toward the elevator. All of them were watching him.

The room was quiet, and then a voice rang out. "May I have a round of applause for my assistant?"

The children broke into wild applause. Newton looked over his shoulder to see who the commotion was for. There was no one else there. All he saw was the elevator door closing behind him, cutting off his escape. The crowd was laughing now, and Newton realized that they had been applauding for him.

He turned to face the room. Way in the back, he saw a woman beckoning to him, waving him forward with her hand.

Newton walked into the room. He now saw that he was in the children's room of the library. The floor was carpeted, and he noticed that someone had painted a mural on a large roll of paper showing a child with a butterfly net running after flying books that looked like butterflies. Under the painting was a sign that said, HOW MANY BOOKS WILL YOU CATCH THIS SPRING?

Newton tiptoed through the children and made his way to the woman in the back. As he got closer, he saw that she was wearing a T-shirt that said, QUIET AND BOOKISH? on the front.

Just as he reached her, she turned around, and he saw that the back of the T-shirt read, NOT BY A LONG SHOT!

The woman picked up a green bedsheet and handed one corner to Newton. She took the other corner and stretched it in front of them like a curtain.

"You're late," she whispered to him behind the sheet.

"What?" said Newton.

"You're late." She looked at him more closely. "Didn't they send you from the school?"

Newton shook his head. "No," he said.

The librarian sighed.

"I know you're too old for story hour," she said, "but I need an assistant to turn the pages of a book and to read out loud while I act the story. It's Butterfly Week, and I'm about to give my first annual performance. What do you say?"

"I really can't stay," said Newton. "I'm kind of in a hurry. I need to find some information about caterpillars."

"Then you've come to the right person. If you help me, I'll help you find anything about caterpillars that you want to know."

Newton peeked around the corner of the sheet. A sea of small faces stared back at him.

"I don't think so," said Newton. "I'm running out of time."

Just then, the elevator door opened. Inside the elevator stood the man in the black hat. The man stuck his head out of the door and surveyed the room.

Newton ducked behind the sheet.

"Okay," said Newton. "I'll help."

"Good," said the woman. "This won't take long. Hold both ends of the sheet. I'm going to change into my costume."

Newton held up the sheet while the woman pulled a bright green T-shirt over the shirt she was already wearing. Quickly, she stepped into a pair of green overalls.

Newton peered out from behind the sheet once more. This time, the elevator door was closing. The man in the black hat was still inside.

Newton felt the woman tap him on the shoulder, and then she grabbed the sheet and swirled it through the air like a cape.

"Ladies and gentlemen, and children of all ages," she called.

The room became quiet, and everyone turned toward her. She continued in a softer voice.

"Welcome to the library. My name is Jasmine Byrd, and I am the new children's librarian in Angel Falls. As you know, this is Butterfly Week. Once a year, and only once a year, during this week I plan to perform *Behold the Butterfly! The Story of the Emerald Rainbow Butterfly*. This year, I will be assisted by . . ."

She turned to Newton. He whispered his name.

"By Mister Newton Bellnap. Newton, take a bow."

Newton bowed low, and everyone clapped.

"As Newton reads the story, I will perform for you my own unique interpretation of the life cycle of the Emerald Rainbow butterfly. Now . . . on with the show!"

She handed Newton a big book, which he opened to the first page. He held the book up so the audience could see the pictures.

"What comes first, the butterfly or the egg?" read Newton. "In our story, we will start with the egg. This is the first stage in the life cycle of a butterfly."

As he spoke, the librarian lowered herself to the floor and curled up into a ball.

The next stage was the larva stage. As Newton read, the librarian poked and pushed her way out of the imaginary egg and stretched out to full length on the floor. Then she began wiggling and slinking her way into the audience.

"Do you know another name for a butterfly larva?" read Newton.

No one in the audience said anything.

"Have you ever seen a caterpillar?" he read.

Everyone nodded their heads.

"Another name for a butterfly larva is a caterpillar."

The librarian got on her knees in the middle of the audience and brought her hands up in front of her mouth. Then she opened and closed her fingers as if they were little jaws.

"Caterpillars are eating machines," read Newton. "They eat and eat and eat all day long."

The librarian bent down and pretended to nibble gently on a little girl's shoulder. The girl giggled in delight.

"The next stage in the caterpillar's life is the pupa. The caterpillar builds a tiny house around its body. A moth caterpillar spins a cocoon, but a butterfly caterpillar creates a chrysalis."

The librarian reached behind her and pulled

out the green sheet, which she now rolled around her entire body, including her head.

"Inside the chrysalis, the caterpillar is changing. Then when it is ready, something new emerges."

There was a commotion inside the sheet. It jumped and bumped, and then Jasmine Byrd reappeared. Slowly she stood, and the sheet dropped away. Gone was the green T-shirt. In its place was a multicolored tie-dyed T-shirt. She stretched out her arms.

"Behold, the butterfly!" read Newton. "From egg to larva to pupa to butterfly. This life cycle of change is called metamorphosis."

The audience broke into thunderous applause. Jasmine Byrd bowed. Then she had Newton take a bow.

"Newton," she said. "You were terrific. Thank you."

"What I really need to know," said Newton, "is what do Emerald Rainbow caterpillars eat?"

"Then you haven't been paying attention," said the librarian. "Didn't you look at the illustrations in the book you just read?"

Actually, Newton hadn't. His mind had been focused on Vanessa the entire time he'd been reading. Now, he grabbed the book once more and opened it.

"Dandelions?" he asked, peering at the illustration. "Emerald Rainbow caterpillars eat dandelions?"

"Dandelion leaves," said the librarian. "Who would have thought that such an elegant insect would feed on a weed found almost everywhere."

She shook his hand.

"Newton, thank you again," she said. "What did the caterpillar say to the butterfly? I never met-a-morphosis I didn't like."

Minutes later Newton stood on the sidewalk below the steps of the library. It was even more crowded now than when he'd come into town. People lined the street, as if they were waiting for something. In the distance, Newton could hear drums and brass and the high-pitched ring of a xylophone. Of course. It was the annual Butterfly Week Parade. He'd forgotten all about it. It was a tradition in Angel Falls. He'd heard about it, but never seen it.

All at once he felt as if someone were watching him. He looked up, and there standing on the top of the library steps, he saw a figure. Newton jumped on his bike, and bending low over the handlebars, rode away as fast as he could.

Behind him on the steps, the man in the black hat stood with his hands on his hips, searching the crowd through his mirrored glasses.

16.

THAT WAS SCRUMPTIOUS

Newton burst into Vanessa's room and flung himself toward the opening under her bed as if he were sliding headfirst into home plate.

"Vanessa, can you hear me?" he called.

He waited for a note to appear, but he heard no rustle of paper, no scratching of pen.

"Vanessa, are you there? I've brought dandelion leaves. They're everywhere. Even in your front yard."

There was still no reply.

"Am I too late?" he wondered. "Did she starve to death while I was gone?"

Newton grabbed a handful of leaves and looked around for the tray he'd had earlier. The tray was nowhere to be seen, but there on the desk was the book he'd tried to give Vanessa earlier as a present, *Magnificent Monsters from the Movies*. He placed the leaves on the book, then slid them under the bed and listened.

"Come on, Vanessa," he whispered to himself. "You can do it."

The sound, when he finally heard it, was soft at first but gradually became louder. It sounded like large insect jaws crunching on something. Newton tried to look under the bed, but it was too dark under there to see what was going on.

"Vanessa, are you still alive?" called Newton.

Finally, he heard something that sounded like a contented sigh. A moment later, a note appeared.

"That was scrumptious!"

The note was followed by something else that slid out from under the bed. Newton looked to see what it was. Then he looked again.

Here were the dandelion leaves, as green as ever. They hadn't been eaten at all. Underneath them was the copy of *Magnificent Monsters from the Movies* that Newton had used as a tray. Only, something was different about it. Newton picked it up.

All that was left was the hard cover of the book. The pages were gone. Newton looked closely at the book's binding. It almost seemed as if someone had carefully cut the pages out with a razor blade . . . or with razor sharp jaws.

Vanessa had eaten the pages right out of the book!

Another note appeared.

"So *that's* what giant Emerald Rainbow caterpillars love best! I'm so glad it isn't dandelion leaves. More! More!"

Newton stared at the remains of the book in his hands. Books? Vanessa wanted to eat books?

Newton looked around the room until he spotted Vanessa's book cases. Her book collection was locked behind glass doors, but there were several other open book shelves full of books. If Vanessa wanted to devour books, then she was in the right place.

Newton pulled down a book and pushed it under the bed. He heard crunching for a few minutes, and then the empty book cover came back out. He slid another book under the bed. More crunching.

Newton fed books to Vanessa for several hours straight. He hadn't realized how hungry she was. He soon learned from looking at the information on the last page of some of the books that she preferred the books that were printed on acid-free and recycled paper, but she would try any book he gave her. Something about the combination of printer's ink on paper was irresistible to her.

After a while he started to relax and call out jokes to her. "'Waiter, waiter, what's this caterpillar doing in my alphabet soup?' 'Don't worry, sir, it's learning to read.'"

Vanessa did not respond, but just kept eating.

Finally, the shelves were empty. Newton heard the pen scratching slowly across paper, and then a note appeared.

"I feel so strange. All I wanted to do before was eat. Now all I want to do is sleep. I think I'll take a little nap. Wake me up in half an hour."

There was silence for a minute, and then Newton heard a new sound. At first he thought it was a cat purring somewhere, but that wasn't quite it. It sounded a little like water bubbling furiously on the stove, but it wasn't a steady sound, it came and went. Finally, he realized what it was.

It was a sound he had never heard before.

It was the sound of a giant green caterpillar — snoring.

17.

PLEASE STEP OUTSIDE
WHILE I CHANGE

Newton spent the next half hour cleaning up the room. There were bits and pieces of left-over food and many uneaten book covers, which he collected and put in a wastebasket. When he was done, he went to wake Vanessa.

He knelt on the floor, lifted up the edge of the covers and peered under the bed. It was dark under there, but he had found a flashlight while he was cleaning.

"Vanessa," he called. "Vanessa?"

There was something under there, but it didn't

look like Vanessa. Newton leaned closer for a better look.

A large, shiny, green object was lying under the bed. The object was long and tubelike, except at the bottom, where it was rounded off as if it were covering a person's shoulders and head. About two-thirds of the way down from the top, a multicolored stripe circled halfway around. Newton's first thought was that the object looked like one of the green pods in *Invasion of the Body Snatchers*. His second thought was that it also looked like the sarcophagus in *The Mummy*.

Vanessa's bed was fairly high off the floor, and there was a lot of room underneath. One end of a short strand of silvery thread was attached to the top of the object, and the other end of the thread was stuck to the underside of the bed. The thread held the top end of the object up in the air and suspended it diagonally so that the bottom portion was touching the floor directly in front of Newton.

Newton sat back on his heels. Somehow he knew that Vanessa was inside that thing. He was also pretty sure he knew what had happened.

"She's reached the pupa stage," he whispered

softly to himself. "A moth caterpillar spins a cocoon, but a butterfly creates a chrysalis. She's a chrysalis."

He had no idea how long it took for a creature to emerge from the pupa stage. And just who or what was going to emerge from this chrysalis? Would it even still be Vanessa? Newton didn't know. There was nothing he could do now but wait.

An hour went by with no change. Another hour passed. Then, just as the grandfather clock downstairs was chiming three o'clock, Newton noticed that the green color of the chrysalis was starting to fade.

Fifteen minutes later, he saw that the chrysalis was becoming transparent. At three-thirty, the green color was entirely gone, and the outer covering was as clear as glass.

Inside, he could see Vanessa lying upside down, her knees pulled up to her chest. She seemed to be covered with a black blanket, and she was sleeping.

Old films of *Snow White*, asleep in her glass coffin after eating the poisoned apple, popped into Newton's mind. The thought of waking Vanessa with a kiss fluttered quickly through his brain, but he didn't think he was ready to catch hold of such an idea and pin it down in reality, so he let it go. He hoped she'd wake up on her own.

Suddenly, there was a crackling sound, and the chrysalis split open at the bottom. Vanessa came tumbling out headfirst and fell to the floor on her back, leaving the rest of the chrysalis still attached to the bed above her. Newton saw that she was soaking wet and still covered with the black blanket.

The fall seemed to wake her up. Slowly she opened her eyes and looked around.

"Newton, is that you?" she asked. "You look upside down."

"So do you," Newton said, "And I have to ask you the same thing. Vanessa, is that you?"

"It's I," said Vanessa. "I mean, I think it is. At least I've got my voice back."

She crawled out from under the bed, wrapping the black blanket tightly around her.

"I'm soaking wet under this thing," she said. "Would you mind if I asked you to please step outside into the hall for a minute while I change?"

Newton left the room and shut the door behind

him. He was only gone a second when he heard a scream from inside the room.

He grabbed the doorknob, but Vanessa yelled, "No, don't come in yet!" He heard another shriek, but it sounded as if Vanessa was laughing, so he waited outside in the hall.

Several minutes later Vanessa called, "Okay, you can come in now, but close your eyes until I count to three." Newton opened the door and walked into the room.

"One," said Vanessa. "Two . . . three."

Newton opened his eyes and stared.

There stood Vanessa. She was wearing blue jeans and a T-shirt. Her hair was still damp and a little frizzy from being towel-dried. It was the same Vanessa he'd met in the field just the other day. But something was different about her.

Something that blew and billowed behind her in the breeze from the open window.

"Wings!" she cried. "I've got wings!"

18.
WiNGS

"**D**on't get too close," warned Vanessa. "They're not dry yet."

The afternoon sun was streaming in through the window, and she stood in its rays, waiting for her wings to dry.

Even though he'd been expecting it, Newton still couldn't believe it was true.

Wings!

Vanessa had wings!

Newton edged a little closer to get a better look, careful not to touch.

The wings looked just like butterfly wings, only

much larger. They appeared to be growing out of the back of Vanessa's shoulders. Each one was in two parts, a top and a bottom, but they overlapped in the middle, and unless you looked closely, they looked like one piece.

The wings' colors were almost exactly the same as the colors of the Emerald Rainbow butterfly: a swirl of multicolor hues on the underside and bright new green on the top.

As Newton watched, he could see the colors get visibly brighter as the wings dried, and he realized that the black blanket he had thought Vanessa had been wrapped in had actually been her wings.

The topmost tips of the wings were a little bit higher than Vanessa's head. The bottoms just missed touching the ground. Vanessa could move her arms and legs normally. They weren't attached to the wings. And when she spread out her arms, the wings stretched out behind her just a bit wider than her widest reach.

"I had the worst time trying to put on this T-shirt," said Vanessa. "It wouldn't go on over my head. I finally had to cut it straight up the back on both sides with scissors, then pin it together with safety pins once I had it on. I may have to cut up all my clothes. Nothing's going to fit any-more."

A little shudder seemed to pass through Vanessa's body. Then suddenly, her wings beat rapidly back and forth, and she shot straight up.

"Ouch!" she cried as her head hit the ceiling.

She immediately fell to the floor in a tangle of arms and legs and wings.

Newton rushed over. "Are you hurt?" he asked.

"I can fly," she whispered. "I can really really fly. It's what I've wanted all my life, and now I can do it."

She stood up and walked to the window.

The window was the old-fashioned kind that opened out from the middle like two tall doors. Just outside the window was a tiny balcony with a railing. Vanessa walked through the open window and out onto the balcony. Newton followed her.

They were on the second floor of the house, about ten feet off the ground. Newton could see what Vanessa had in mind, and he was about to say to her, "I think if this were a movie, this would be the part where someone turns to the camera and says, 'Kids, don't try this at home.'" But before he could say anything, Vanessa had climbed up on the black iron railing, balanced precariously for a second or two, and then launched herself into space.

Her wings beat furiously back and forth, and then . . .

She flew.

Up she went in a halting, jerking, start-and-stop motion, almost as if she were jumping up a long flight of stairs. Each upward bounce brought a whoop or a shriek of delight. When she reached the top of the tallest tree in her backyard, she spread her wings wide and glided back down to the balcony.

"It's the best, Newton!" she cried. "Oh, I knew it, I knew it, I knew it! It's the best!"

"Doesn't it feel weird — having wings?" asked Newton.

"Weird? No! It's wonderful!"

Then she was gone again, skimming low over the backyard and up into the sky. This time her flight was a little smoother. Once again, she returned to Newton on the balcony.

"You've got to try it with me," she said.

Newton looked down at the ground below, and his grip involuntarily tightened on the railing.

"You know me," he said. "My feet are planted firmly on the ground."

"You've said that before," said Vanessa. "But now that I know you a little better, I think that secretly your head may be in the clouds."

Vanessa turned her head suddenly and looked back at the house.

"Did you hear that?" she asked. "What was that sound?" She cupped her hand over her ear as if to hear better.

Newton turned to face the house. He hadn't heard a thing. He was wondering what Vanessa could have heard, when all of a sudden he felt someone grab the back of his belt.

"It's adventure calling!" yelled Vanessa.

The next thing Newton knew, his feet were no longer planted firmly on anything, and he felt himself being dragged over the edge of the balcony.

"Vanessa, wait! Stop! What are you doing?" he cried.

"Don't worry, Newton," she yelled back as the ground spun farther and farther away below them. "You're going to love this!"

19.
ADVENTURE CALLING

"Whoooooaaaaa!" yelled Newton as Vanessa headed straight up into the sky.

He flailed his arms and kicked his feet, which made Vanessa jerk to the right or the left with each movement.

When she reached the top of the tall tulip tree in her backyard, she tried to level off, but Newton was twisting and turning so much that she misjudged her height and ended up dragging him through the topmost leaves and branches.

A robin shot up from its nest and looked at them in surprise as they flew by.

"Newton, stop squirming!" yelled Vanessa. "You'll make me drop you!"

Newton heard her and immediately stopped moving, but he hung folded almost in two at the waist from where she held the back of his belt. His body felt like a sack of cement, but his head was so dizzy, it felt as light as a pillowcase full of feathers.

"Try to straighten out your body," called Vanessa as she skimmed over the treetops. "Stretch out your arms and legs as if you were floating on water. I'm doing all the work. You don't have to do anything but enjoy this. Try to have fun!"

But Newton wasn't having fun. The belt cut into his stomach, and he was sure that any minute he was going to fall.

"Newton, look up ahead," called Vanessa. "See that old tree that doesn't have all its leaves yet? The one that has five branches sprouting up from one point at the top? I'm going to set you down there for a moment. Are you ready?"

Newton looked. The branches of the tree reached up almost like an upturned hand. From Newton's point of view the branches seemed to be hurtling toward him ready to strike. Then

Vanessa slowed, and hovering almost motionless above the tree, she set him gently down into the branches as if she were placing him in a giant's outstretched palm.

Only when she was sure that he was safe from falling did she let go. Then she landed gracefully on one of the branches. If Newton hadn't known better he would have thought she'd been doing this all her life.

"I've got an idea," she said.

"Vanessa," said Newton. "I've had enough of your brilliant ideas. I don't want to die before I get to be a teenager. Take me down to the ground now!"

"But Newton," said Vanessa, "I've got an idea for a way to hook you up so you can't possibly fall."

"Take me down now! I mean it! Take me down, and I'll walk home."

"Newton, life isn't a movie. You can't spend your whole life watching things, you've got to take part. This is an adventure. It's something I've wanted all my life, and I want to share it with you. Now wait here. I'll be right back."

With a rush of wings she was gone.

Newton held on to the tree so tightly that he

began to shake all over. It felt like hours before Vanessa returned.

He heard her before he saw her.

She was clanking and jangling as if she were carrying chains. As she landed on the branch, Newton saw why.

"It's one of the swings from the backyard," she said. "It took a while to figure out how to unhook it. This is going to be great."

Each side of the swing seat had a metal ring with a chain attached. The other end of each chain had a hook with a spring clip attachment. Vanessa took the top end of the right-side chain, threaded it through the belt loop on the right side of her jeans, and then brought it back down and clipped it to the ring on the right side of the swing. She threaded the left-side chain through the belt loop on the left side of her jeans and attached the end to the left side of the swing.

With Vanessa giving directions, Newton sat in the swing seat and took off his belt. Then he put it on again, this time threading it through links in the chain on either side of him.

"Just like a seat belt," said Vanessa. "This should be a lot more comfortable than before."

She handed him a book of maps that she had picked up back at the house.

"I'll fly, you navigate," she said. "Feel free to point out any areas of scenic interest. Now . . . hold on tight!"

20.

WHO *ARE* THOSE GUYS?

"**B**lue sky, here we come!" cried Vanessa.

And they were off again, with Newton suspended in the swing about six feet below Vanessa. It was a little awkward at first, but after a few moments, they got the hang of it.

Once again, Vanessa headed straight up. Then she turned and dived, pulling up just above tree level and gliding along over the tops of the trees.

Newton tried to have fun, and after a while he began to relax a little and enjoy the view, but secretly, deep down, he was still terrified.

"I went on a roller coaster with my parents

once," he called to Vanessa. "This reminds me of that time. I thought it was going to be fun, but my mother kept saying, 'Just hang on, just hang on,' so that's what I tried to do."

"Newton, this is an adventure!" yelled Vanessa. "You don't need to always hang on so tightly. Try to let go a little. When I count to three, I want you to scream as loudly as you can."

"What if someone hears?" said Newton, but Vanessa had already headed up into the sky again, higher than they'd yet been.

"Get ready," she called. "One . . . two . . . three!"

Once again she dived for the treetops.

Newton screamed at the top of his lungs. It seemed to help. He was still terrified, and yet maybe it was possible, he decided, to enjoy this moment after all.

Together they soared over the canopy of green, and Newton noticed for the first time that the treetops looked a little like rolling green hills. He saw, too, that there were gaps in the canopy, and he could occasionally see all the way to the ground, where gray roads crisscrossed the land-scape, and objects cast long shadows in the late afternoon sun.

"Vanessa," he shouted, "we better make sure

nobody sees us. We'd have an awful lot of explaining to do."

"No one will see us," yelled Vanessa. "Besides, even if they did, we're so far up they wouldn't be able to tell who or what we are. They'd probably just think we were some strange kind of butterfly."

She swooped low again.

"Look, there's the field where I first found you." A clearing of bright green new grass opened up below them.

"And look," said Vanessa. "There are the butterflies. They're still migrating."

She flew around the four corners of the field and then joined the band of butterflies, heading northwest. She flew just a little above them, so as not to disturb their journey.

"Do you think they know we're their friends?" asked Vanessa.

An instant later her question seemed to be answered when the butterflies below them changed the pattern of their flight and rose to surround them. In twos and threes, some of them began to land on Newton's arms and legs, until he was covered with them.

"I think they're saying hello," yelled Newton.

He looked down to see if more were coming, and that's when he spotted the car. It was traveling on a road just below them, keeping pace with their flight. Newton couldn't see who was driving or how many people were in the car.

"Vanessa, I think we're being followed," he called.

Vanessa looked down, saw the car, and immediately began evasive action.

"Good-bye butterflies," she said, and then swooped up and away to the left. The car disappeared under the trees.

"That should take care of that," she said.

Newton looked down, and for a split second he could see through a gap in the treetops. The car had turned onto a different road and was still following, directly below them.

"They're still there," said Newton.

Vanessa turned left again. Now they were traveling southeast, exactly opposite to the way they had been flying when they had spotted the butterflies. Sure enough, they looked below them and saw wave after wave of butterflies flying in the opposite direction. Newton scanned the ground, and there, once again, was the car, still keeping pace with them.

"Who *are* those guys?" he asked. It was a line he remembered from *Butch Cassidy and the Sundance Kid*.

"I recognize the car," said Vanessa. "I'm pretty sure it's just one person — that butterfly collector we met in the field the other day. I thought we could lose him, but he seems smarter than I thought."

"This is the third time I've run into him today," said Newton. "He keeps asking about you, but I haven't told him anything. Do you think he can tell who we are?"

"No, we're up too high to see clearly, but he's awfully persistent. I don't want to end up as the prize trophy in his collection."

"Look!" said Newton. "Something's happening to the butterflies."

There was a sudden shift in the ranks of the butterfly migration below them. One minute the butterflies were flying at treetop level, the next minute they had drifted lower, until they were flying just above the surface of the road.

Newton and Vanessa watched as row after row of butterflies flying in one direction met the car traveling in the opposite direction. Instantly, the windshield was covered with butterflies.

The car was not going fast enough to hurt the insects, and now it slowed even further as more and more butterflies landed on its surface.

"That will take care of him," said Vanessa. "He can't see where he's going."

But she spoke too soon, for suddenly the windshield wipers turned on, gently sweeping the butterflies away. The car speeded up, but all of a sudden a plume of white steam shot from the front, and the car rolled to a stop.

"What happened?" asked Newton as they flew away.

"The butterflies covered the radiator and it overheated," said Vanessa. "I've heard of it happening before during migrations, but I've never seen it myself. It was almost as if the butterflies were trying to help us."

Newton looked back down the road at the car, which was fading in the distance. Beside it he could see the figure of a man who appeared to be jumping up and down and waving at them . . . a man who was wearing a black baseball hat and mirrored sunglasses.

21.

WHAT VANESSA FOUND

The next morning after breakfast Newton raced over to Vanessa's house on his bike. Once again, no one answered the doorbell, and he let himself in. But when he got to her room, she was not there.

On her desk was a note.

Dear Newton,
I did a lot of thinking last night. It wasn't fair of me to make you fly when you weren't ready. There's something I have to look for, and I

think it's best if I do it on my own. Don't wait around for me, I'm not sure when I'll be back.

The note was signed, "Sincerely," but that had been crossed out and replaced with "Your friend, Vanessa."

Newton didn't know what to do. He wandered around Vanessa's room trying to think. Flying had been one of the most terrifying things he had ever done. And yet . . . and yet, he had survived.

Looking back on it now, flying also felt like the most exciting and adventurous thing he had ever done. And one of the things he had liked about it had been sharing the adventure with another person. They had done it as a team. So why had Vanessa deserted him to go out flying on her own? He walked back to the desk and gave it a little kick of annoyance, nearly knocking over the half-full jar of green powder that still sat there, almost glowing in the morning light.

"How does it really work?" he wondered. "Did she rub it on her arms like she said she was going to? Or did she eat it?"

He didn't know the answer, and he wasn't sure he wanted to find out for himself. He looked around the room one more time. Then he went home.

During the last couple of days Newton had gotten so used to doing things with Vanessa that now he wasn't sure how to spend the time alone. So, he made a list of things to do and spent the rest of the morning working on them. First, he looked up "Vanessa" and "Atalanta" in his sisters' unabridged dictionary and in the encyclopedia, just to see what they really meant. He even looked up "Zephyr," and decided it fit Vanessa perfectly. Then he finished reading the Edgar Allan Poe assignment, wrote a two-page summary of *The Purloined Letter* for English class, and washed the family car. His parents, who hadn't seen much of him all week, remarked to themselves that he seemed . . . thoughtful.

That afternoon, just after lunch, Newton decided to go on a short bike ride. Somehow, the road took him past Vanessa's house.

"Where is she?" he wondered. "What has she gone to find?"

Just then, he heard the sound of a breeze rustle through the new leaves on the trees, and a moment later he saw a shape silhouetted against the sky. The shape landed on the balcony outside Vanessa's window. Then Newton heard a word that sounded like, "Ouch," as the shape went inside and banged the upper tip of its right wing on the top edge of the window.

It was Vanessa's voice.

Newton left his bike on the lawn and ran up to the house. The front door was unlocked, as always.

"Vanessa," he said as he burst into her room. "You went flying without me!" He meant it to sound somewhat playful, but as the words came out, even he could hear that he sounded annoyed.

"Newton, have you been waiting for me all day?" asked Vanessa. "There was something I had to look for, and I had to do it on my own."

She walked over to the window and closed it. Then she turned to face Newton.

"Haven't you ever had to read that Kipling poem that goes, '*She* travels the fastest who travels alone'? Besides, you were really scared yesterday, and I realized I had no right trying to make you fly before you were ready."

"I was ready," said Newton.

"No, Newton. I pushed you. I thought about it later, and I felt like a mother bird trying to push a baby bird out of its nest before it's ready to fly."

"I thought something terrible might have happened to you today," said Newton.

"Something certainly happened," said Vanessa. "Sit down and let me tell you what I found."

Vanessa sat on a corner of her bed and Newton sat on the floor.

"Last night," she began, "I hardly slept at all. First of all, my father knocked on the door when I was getting ready for bed and asked if I was all right. I managed to just poke my head around the edge of the door and told him I was changing and couldn't come out, but that I was fine. That seemed to satisfy him. I hope he doesn't suspect something. He usually doesn't seem interested in how I am.

"Then, have you ever imagined what it's like trying to sleep in a bed when you have wings? I thought I'd be able to wrap them around me like a bathrobe, but when I tried to go to sleep they stood up together, straight over my back. All I could see was the rainbow part underneath. The green tops came together in the middle. I had to roll onto my stomach. I guess it's the same way butterflies sleep. It's kind of awkward, but I suppose it's the price you pay for having wings.

"Anyway, there I was in bed on my stomach with my wings pointing straight up in the air, and I started to wonder, am I the only one who has wings? Am I the only one in the whole world like me?

"I've never thought about stuff like that before, but that's what I thought about all night long. One minute I'd be happy because now I can fly. Then the next minute I'd think — I like being unique, but I'm not sure I want to be the only one who has wings. I wondered if I had the courage to be that different. I went around and around like that in my mind all night long, and finally I thought that maybe there are others like me somewhere.

"So this morning, as soon as it started to get light, I wrote you that note. Then I went out to try my wings on my own and to look for others with wings.

"I started out over Ruth Ann's house. Remember you said you saw someone with green hair? I thought maybe she had gone through the same thing I had, but no one was home at her house.

"I flew all morning. Strangely enough, I didn't get tired. These wings are strong. I flew for miles. I looked everywhere, but I didn't find any others. And then, after I'd flown as far as I could and seen all I could see, I realized I had found something after all. I found that I'm a thing. A thing with wings. It's who I am, and I like it. I like being able to fly, and it doesn't matter if there are others or if I'm all alone."

"But Vanessa," said Newton. "You're not alone. I'm still your friend. Besides, how can you know after only one day — there may be others."

"Wait," said Vanessa. "There's more. I'm not finished, yet.

"When it got to be noon, I headed for home. At first I'd thought, 'Why go home at all? Why not just stay out all day and fly off into the sunset?' But I realized that only works in books and movies. You can't fly off into the sunset in real life. So I decided to come back.

"I was almost home, flying low over the butterfly garden one more time, when I noticed something I hadn't seen before. Way in a far corner of the garden, camouflaged by green leaves, I spotted a building shaped like a dome. It seemed to be made out of window screen material, and it was as tall as a three-story house.

"I flew down, and as I got closer, I could see through the screen. Newton, you'll never believe what I saw. It wasn't just a dome, it was a giant cage. Inside there were rows and rows of hospital beds, and in each bed was a giant green caterpillar!

"When I got right up against the screen I saw that there were medical charts with names at the foot of each bed. And the first name I saw was Ruth Ann Harbinger!

"Newton, Ruth Ann isn't with some specialist, like her mother said. Ruth Ann is there in that cage! And she's not the only one. Nearly everyone from our class in school is there! They've all been going through the exact same thing I have, and I never knew it.

"Not one of them has changed into a butterfly, though. Most of them are just lying on their beds and staring up into the air. They don't look good at all. I called through the screen and tried to talk to them, but they didn't respond. I didn't see any food around. I think they might be starving to death.

"I don't know who is keeping them there, or why, or what they plan to do with them. All I know is someone has to rescue them, and I'm the only one who can do it.

"Newton, I'm going back to that place to rescue everybody, and I'm going there right now!"

22.
TO THE RESCUE

Vanessa jumped up and grabbed her back-pack.

"I'm ready," she said. "Let's go."

But Newton hung back.

"Wait a minute," he said. "What exactly are you planning to do?"

"I'm planning to do the exact same thing that you did for me," said Vanessa. "First, I have to get some books. Then, I have to take them to the cage so the kids don't starve. After that, I'll just have to wing it . . . so to speak."

"And where are you going to get these books?" asked Newton. "You've eaten yours."

"There are other books downstairs," said Vanessa.

"And how are you going to explain to your father when all those books disappear?"

Vanessa sat back down.

"What about at your house?" she asked.

"We have a lot of movies, but not many books. Besides, I think I know where there's a bigger and closer supply."

Newton turned his head slowly until he was looking at . . .

"Newton Bellnap, don't even think about it!" cried Vanessa, as she literally flew across the room and threw herself in front of the tall bookcase with the glass doors. "My children's books are off limits!"

"But I thought you wanted to rescue your friends."

"I do, but not with these."

"Why not? They don't look like antiques. Some of them are paperbacks. They can't be very expensive. Your collection can't be worth much."

"Newton, I can't believe you don't know the difference between something that's expensive and something that's valuable. In terms of money this collection probably isn't worth much to anyone. But it's still valuable to me."

"But why?" asked Newton. "You could replace all these books with new ones tomorrow. What's so special about these books?"

Vanessa sighed. And when she spoke, it was with a touch of sadness mixed with pride.

"They were my mother's," she said slowly. "I can just barely remember her reading them to me when I was a little girl. Later, when I learned to read, these were the first books I turned to. I still remember exactly where I was when I read each one. I've read them all over and over since then until they've become a part of me. This is where I got my love of flying. My mother passed it on to me through her books. They're all I have left of her. How can I give them up?"

Newton was silent for a moment. Then he spoke.

"Vanessa, when you're at school, when you're at the library, even when you're flying, where are your books?"

"Right here in my room, safely on the shelf, behind glass doors."

"No," said Newton. "They're here," he tapped

his forehead, "in your mind. You just said so yourself — your books have become a part of you. That's the thing about books. They live on in the people who have read them. As long as you're alive, these books can't be destroyed. The things in this bookcase are only paper. The real books are in your mind — and here, in your heart."

Newton continued.

"I'm not saying you should throw your books away or give them up to just anyone, but your friends need them. Think of it as a donation to a worthy cause. These books helped you to fly. Let them help someone else."

Vanessa turned away from Newton. She faced the bookcase and stared at the books for a moment. Then she unlocked the locks on the glass doors.

The doors sprang open.

"Okay," she said, turning back to face Newton. "I'll do it. I'll use my books. I just have one question."

"What's that?" asked Newton.

"That was a great speech you just gave. But you're not a book person. Where did you learn so much about books?"

Newton smiled.

"In a movie," he said. "*Fahrenheit 451*."

"Of course," said Vanessa. "Where else? I should have known."

They yanked the top sheet off Vanessa's bed and piled the books onto it. Newton pulled the four corners together and tied them to form a giant sack.

"Do you think this will be enough books?" he asked. "Judging from what you ate, those caterpillars are going to be really hungry."

"We have to start somewhere," said Vanessa. "This is the best we can do for now."

They opened the window and walked out onto the balcony. Vanessa hooked up the swing, and Newton strapped himself on. Then, with Newton holding on to the overflowing sack of books, away they went into the early afternoon sky.

They kept low, just brushing the tops of the trees, to avoid being seen. They flew over the field, and over the woods, and over the wall that surrounded the garden.

"Look, over there," said Vanessa.

Newton looked to where she was pointing, and there in the far corner of the garden he saw it — the dome.

It was in a part of the garden they hadn't explored, and it was exactly the way Vanessa had described it. The building was circular. The side walls were solid and went straight up for about ten feet. From the top of these, metal braces arched up to meet in the center, forming a dome that was covered with wire mesh screening.

Green leaves had been pushed through the screen, making it difficult to see the dome from the air, unless you knew exactly where to look.

Vanessa and Newton swooped low over the dome. From the hospital beds on the floor below, thirty faces stared up at them. Thirty faces of thirty giant green caterpillars.

"Newton," said Vanessa. "Do you see that flat platform at the very top of the dome? I'm going to land there. Get ready."

She hovered over the dome and slowly lowered Newton onto the platform where the metal braces met in the center. Newton let go of the sack, then unbuckled his seat belt and carefully stepped down. He quickly dropped to his hands and knees and looked around.

The platform was a little larger than he'd expected and fairly flat.

Vanessa landed next to him.

"Watch out," she said. "We've got to do this before someone sees us." She set her backpack down on the platform and began rummaging inside.

Newton spoke. "I don't think you could possibly have anything in that bag that would help us now," he said. "What do you plan to do — cut through the wires with a birthday cake?"

"Newton, I'm surprised at you," said Vanessa. "You're the movie expert. What's always baked inside a birthday cake in every prison escape movie you've ever seen?"

"A file?"

"Well, I don't have a file, but here's the next best thing." She handed him a pair of wire-cutting pliers. "I told you, I like to be prepared. Start cutting."

Snip! Snip! Snip!

To Newton's surprise, the screening cut quite easily. In less than a minute he had cut away a long section and pushed it away from the center platform.

Vanessa waited while he grabbed her backpack and the sack of books and scrambled back onto the swing. Then she slowly descended through the opening in the dome, taking care not to cut her wings on the sharp edges of the screen. A moment later they touched down on a hardwood floor.

Newton had expected that the caterpillars would react in some way when they saw the rescuers, but they didn't move at all. They just lay on their backs in their hospital beds, staring upward.

"They're in worse shape than I realized," said Vanessa. "I hope we're not too late."

Newton and Vanessa each grabbed a stack of books and started walking along the rows of beds.

Newton stopped next to a bed and held out a book. The caterpillar in the bed didn't move. Newton waved the book gently in front of the caterpillar's face, hoping it would see or maybe smell the book, but the caterpillar still didn't respond.

Newton leaned forward to see if the caterpillar was still alive, and as he did, something tapped him on the back.

He turned and saw that the caterpillar in the bed behind him had extended his arm and was slowly, painfully, reaching for a book. Newton gave it *The Chrysalids* by John Wyndham.

Something tapped Newton on the back again, and he turned to find the first caterpillar also extending a short insect arm toward him. He gave it *Pilgrimage* by Zenna Henderson.

Soon all the caterpillars had books in their claws. Some even had reached out and grabbed books with each of their six arms. The sound of munching filled the air.

Newton and Vanessa ran up and down the rows of beds as fast as they could, passing out books and picking up the uneaten parts. The mountain of books they had brought quickly dwindled until finally Vanessa said, "This is the last one."

She held it up for Newton to see — *Peter Pan*.

"You could keep that one," said Newton. "I know how much it means to you. Maybe you could use it like a seed. Let it be the start of a whole new collection."

"No," said Vanessa, handing it to the closest hungry caterpillar. "They need it more than I do."

Together they walked down the rows one more time. The caterpillars were still hungry.

"We don't have enough books," said Vanessa. "What are we going to do now?" She turned to Newton, but he was no longer walking beside her. He had stopped and was kneeling beside one of the beds.

"Look at this," he said. He reached under the bed and pulled out a white cardboard carton. It was full of books. He reached under another bed and dragged out a carton exactly like the first. It, too, was full of books.

"What's going on here?" asked Vanessa, as Newton pulled more cartons out from under the beds. "There are plenty of books here. Why didn't someone give them to the caterpillars? The caterpillars are too weak to find them on their own."

It was a question they couldn't answer. Once again they grabbed stacks of books and fed them to the caterpillars, until one by one the caterpillars began to fall asleep.

As Newton fed one last book to one last caterpillar, he heard Vanessa say to herself, "I've done all I can do. Now there's nothing to do but wait."

23.

SEVERAL HOURS LATER

The scene at the dome was quite different several hours later. The books had worked their magic. The caterpillars were gone, and in their place were rows of chrysalises.

Some of the chrysalises had already begun to open, and Newton and Vanessa were busy, running up and down the rows, checking on each one. Newton had found clothes under all the beds, and he'd set these out so that everyone would have something to wear. Now he stopped at a chrysalis that was completely empty.

"What happened to this one?" he asked, moving closer for a better look. "There's no one here."

"Look out below!" called a voice.

Newton and Vanessa turned their heads to look up, and as they did, there was a frantic flapping sound like pieces of wet paper beating against the air, and something came crashing and tumbling downward toward them from above.

Some thing . . .

With wings.

The figure hit the floor and rolled to a stop in front of them in a confusion of arms, legs, and wings.

For a minute, Newton and Vanessa couldn't see who it was, and then the creature sat up and spoke.

"Vanessa, have you got a Band-Aid? I think I've torn the edge of my left wing tip. These wings are totally O.O.C."

"Ruth Ann!" cried Vanessa. She turned to Newton. "It's Ruth Ann Harbinger! She always makes a dramatic entrance."

Newton had never met Ruth Ann Harbinger before. He saw now that she was short and kind of skinny, and she was wearing black denim bib overalls that fastened with straps across her back.

Tied in a bow at the back of her hair was a pink ribbon.

From her shoulders sprouted a pair of wings exactly like Vanessa's — bright green on top, and rainbow colored underneath. The left wing had a slight rip at the edge of the top half. Vanessa had reached into her backpack and was now trying to stick the wing back together with a Band-Aid.

"You looked kind of busy," Ruth Ann was telling Vanessa. "So I decided to try out these wings and surprise you."

Vanessa didn't seem to be about to introduce him, so Newton decided to introduce himself.

"My name's Newton," he said.

"I'm pleased to meet you, Newt," said Ruth Ann. She turned to Vanessa. "He's K.O.C.," she whispered loudly.

Vanessa just rolled her eyes.

"What are O.O.C. and K.O.C.?" asked Newton.

"Out of Control," said Ruth Ann. "I guess my wings aren't completely dry, yet. K.O.C. means, well . . . Kind Of Cute."

Vanessa interrupted. "What I want to know is, what's going on? How did you get here, Ruth Ann?"

"Sit down," said Ruth Ann, "and let me tell

you." So Newton and Vanessa sat on the floor and listened as Ruth Ann told her story.

"The last thing I remember," said Ruth Ann, "was that I was trying to call you. I wanted to apologize . . ."

Vanessa cut her off with a wave of her hand. "Apology accepted," she said.

Ruth Ann continued.

"I got so tired I couldn't keep my eyes open. I must have fallen asleep right where I was, in that big leather chair we have downstairs. The next thing I knew, I woke up here, in a giant dome-covered space full of hospital beds, and in each bed there was a giant bug. I tried to get up to run out, but I quickly learned, I was a bug, too. No wonder no one came to my birthday party. The same thing was happening to all of us.

"I was starving, but there wasn't anything to eat. I lost all track of time because I kept falling asleep, but I finally realized I was in big 'T' — that's big Trouble — and I decided I had to escape. I rolled off the bed. Then I crawled to the door.

"To my surprise, it was wide open. I could see down a short hallway to another door that led outside, and that door was open, too. There must be a giant fan hidden somewhere in the hallway between the two doors because it blew a continuous blast of warm air through the doors into the dome. I guess the wind from the fan would catch a flying creature by its wings and send it tumbling backward. There was no way a thing with wings could escape, but it didn't affect a crawling thing like me at all.

"No one was around. I crawled out of the building and found that I was in a far corner of the garden. I wanted to get as far away from the dome as I could, so I kept moving. Imagine my surprise, Vanessa, when I heard your voice."

"You must have been near the butterfly tree when Newton and I had our picnic," said Vanessa. "You were the one who made that noise we heard in the grass. We thought you were a snake."

"I tried to reach you," said Ruth Ann. "But you ran away. I finally got so tired and hungry that I just curled up into a ball.

"I kept falling asleep and waking up. I don't know how long I was out in the garden, but someone must have found me and brought me back because I finally woke up back here in the dome.

I don't remember too much after that, except that someone finally gave me something to eat, and when I woke up — I had wings!"

"That's the exact same thing that happened to me," said Vanessa. She looked at Newton. "Sort of," she added.

By now all of the chrysalises had opened, and figures were sitting or standing, looking slightly confused as their wings unfolded in the light of the slowly setting sun.

"We've got to get out of here now," said Vanessa. "Even if everyone's wings aren't completely dry."

She pointed up to the hole in the roof.

"That's the way out!" she called. "You're free! Come on! We're taking you home."

There was a sudden *whoosh* and almost at once, twenty-nine large pairs of wings beat the air and lifted upward. One by one, the things flew through the opening in the screen and out into the still bright early evening sky.

"That was easier than I expected," said Ruth Ann, as she, Vanessa, and Newton watched from the floor of the dome.

"Too easy," said Vanessa.

"I think we'd better . . ." said Newton, but his

voice was cut off by a piercing scream that split the air.

"What's that?" asked Vanessa.

"It's an alarm," said Ruth Ann. "They've spotted us. We've got to get out of here B.O.H."

"What's B.O.H.?" asked Newton.

"Like a Bat Outta . . ."

"Help!" cried Newton, as Vanessa in one smooth motion grabbed him by the belt loops on his pants, pushed him into the swing seat, and lifted him straight up out of the dome and into the cloud of wings circling above them.

"Follow me!" Vanessa called to the others, and she abruptly changed direction, zooming up and back toward the middle of the garden.

The shriek of the alarm began to fade as they flew across the garden and approached the wall, but now a new sound started, wafting up from somewhere among the trees on the other side of the wall. Newton was the first to hear it.

"What's that?" he called up to Vanessa.

Vanessa listened for a moment.

"It's just our wings," she yelled back. "Don't you love that sound?"

Newton listened again. Yes, he did like the way

all those giant wings sounded, but what was that other sound? It was a lot like wings, but different. There was something familiar about it, and it seemed to be getting closer.

Newton looked up and saw that Vanessa had heard it. She looked worried.

They had almost reached the wall. Beyond it were the woods. If they could reach the woods, Newton thought, they might be able to hide somewhere, but the sound was coming from just on the other side of the wall. Whatever was making it was between them and safety.

Newton looked at Vanessa. Suddenly her eyes went wide, and he realized she knew what the sound was.

"Turn!" she yelled. "Everybody turn! Now!"

Thirty-one pairs of wings turned on her command, and just in time. For there, rising slowly from behind the wall was a giant flying object that blocked their path.

"Come down!" cried a voice from the flying object. "Come down at once!"

24.
THE CHASE

"**I**t's a helicopter!" cried Vanessa.

A wash of air from the rotating blades blasted them violently sideways, and Newton nearly fell from the swing.

"We've got to get away from the rotors," called Ruth Ann. "We can't fly in the wind they're making."

Newton looked around him. Things with wings were tumbling through the air in uncontrolled flight. He looked back over his shoulder, and for a split second he could see through the glass bubble in the helicopter. There, sitting next to the pilot, was the man in the black hat.

Another blast hit Newton, and he felt himself being torn from the swing.

"Hang on!" yelled Vanessa. "Hang on!"

Suddenly, from behind him, Newton heard a change in the sound from the helicopter. It seemed to be growing fainter.

The air grew calmer.

Then the helicopter was gone.

"That was close," called Vanessa. "We've got to get out of here before it comes back."

"But we still have a long way to go," said Ruth Ann. "There's no way we can outfly that machine. It's much faster than we are. It'll catch us for sure."

"We'll just have to try," said Vanessa. "At any rate, let's get as far as we can before it catches us. Maybe we'll find a way out of this yet. Try to think like a butterfly."

They regrouped in midair. Vanessa and Ruth Ann led the way, with Newton dangling below.

"Vanessa," said Newton. "I don't suppose you have something in your backpack that can save us now."

Vanessa didn't answer for a moment, and then Newton's swing lurched violently in midair.

"My backpack!" cried Vanessa. "I left it at the dome. I've got to go back."

"You can't go back now," said Ruth Ann. "It's too dangerous. You'll have to wait."

Just then, they heard the chopping beat of rotors, and they knew that the helicopter had found them again. This time it kept a respectful distance behind them so they weren't bothered by the downdraft from the rotors, but it stuck to their trail.

"We have to shake that thing," said Vanessa. "If it sees where we go, it'll wait till we land, then just swoop down and catch us. If there were only someplace we could hide."

"Yeah, right," said Ruth Ann. "Tell me where a group of thirty-one kids with giant brightly colored wings plus one riding on a swing is going to hide."

Newton looked down.

He could see that they were rapidly approaching the field where he'd first talked to Vanessa. He had a feeling that in another minute they'd fly over the clearing and he'd see himself as he'd been that day, sitting under the tree and reading . . . and reading. . . .

That was it!

What had Edgar Allan Poe said in *The Purloined Letter*? The best place to hide is in plain sight.

Newton looked back. If only the helicopter would stay well behind them for the next sixty seconds, they might have a chance.

He called up to Vanessa.

"I think there's a way we can hide from that thing," he yelled. "I've got a plan. We'll have to do it fast, and we'll have to do it all together."

Quickly the plan was passed back and forth to all the flyers. Then, as the group reached the line of trees that marked the edge of the woods and the beginning of the field, they soared straight up into the sky as if they were one butterfly. At the top of their flight they rested for an instant.

Then, in one single motion, they swooped straight down behind the trees and vanished from sight.

25.

THANK YOU, EDGAR ALLAN POE

Newton couldn't breathe.

There was something in his mouth.

High overhead he could hear a helicopter searching for thirty-one things with wings. He could imagine what the pilot was thinking.

One minute they had been there. The next minute they were gone.

The helicopter kept crisscrossing the field, but it was obvious there was no one there. After a while it moved away to search the woods again. The sound of the rotors grew fainter and fainter, and finally it disappeared altogether.

Newton spit out a mouthful of grass — bright green, new spring grass. Then, he rolled over, pushed aside the thing that was covering him, and sat up.

"O.U.C.H.," said Ruth Ann.

"What does that stand for?" asked Newton.

"It stands for ouch! Be careful with my wing. It has enough rips in it already."

Newton looked around.

He was sitting in the middle of the open field.

Lying next to him on her stomach was Ruth Ann, her wings spread flat against the ground. On the other side was Vanessa, her wings also flat against the ground. Next to her was someone from school, and next to him was someone else. They were all lying in the field, all in plain sight, and all invisible in the fading evening light.

The tops of their wings were all spring green, the exact same color as the new grass that covered the field. They could not be spotted from the air because the color of their wing-tops blended in so well with the color of their surroundings.

"Newt, you saved us," said Ruth Ann. She called out to Vanessa. "Is he some kind of genius or something?"

"No," said Vanessa. "I just told him to think like

a butterfly, and that's exactly what he did. This is a perfect example of 'camouflage' and 'protective coloration.' This is the same way that butterflies hide from their predators."

But Newton wasn't really listening. All he could think was, "Thank you, Edgar Allan Poe. If I hadn't finished reading *The Purloined Letter*, then we all would have been caught."

"Earth to Newton, Earth to Newton, come in please," said Vanessa, tapping him on the head.

Newton jumped.

"Look," she said, "I'm going to fly this flock over to my house. It's just a few minutes away. No one will ever think of looking for them there. I think you should head for your home now. You're not that fond of flying anyway, and it's an easy walk to your house from here."

She turned back to the group, and one by one they sprang into the air. Vanessa was the last to go.

"Isn't it great, Newton!" she said. "This morning I thought I was the only one. And now, look. I'm not alone. Everybody has wings."

She lifted off gracefully and flew to the front of the group. There was a soft rush of wings. Then they were gone.

Newton walked across the field and out to the road.

"Everybody but me," he whispered to himself.

He was not exactly happy with this turn of events. Yes, he was glad not to be dangling from a swing a hundred feet in the air, but he wanted to be included in whatever was going to happen next.

"She's not alone," he muttered. "Of course she's not alone. When has she ever been alone through any of this? I've been right there every step of the way. I'm not leaving now just because she's finally found a lot of friends who are just like her. Besides . . . my bike is at her house."

So, instead of turning back to his own house, he turned toward hers and began to walk.

When he reached Vanessa's lawn, he picked up his bike and stood looking up at her bedroom window. Were they all up there now, crowded into the room, having a party? Should he walk up to the house, or would it be better simply to turn and ride home?

He was standing there, trying to make up his mind, when a car came hurtling down the road behind him. It turned a corner on screeching tires, and then flew up the driveway in a spray of gravel and dust.

The car lurched to a stop at the front door, and a figure jumped out. Newton could see that it was a man — a man who wore a black baseball hat and mirrored sunglasses.

And then Newton saw something that sent a chill through his entire body. Clutched in one hand, the man held Vanessa's backpack!

With two leaping steps the man reached the front door. Newton thought he would stop to knock, but instead, the man threw open the door and jumped into the front hallway.

For a moment the man stood there, silhouetted against the light from the open doorway like a diagram of doom. Then he ran up the stairs in the front hallway and disappeared from sight.

26.

THE MAN IN THE HAT COMES BACK

For a second Newton stood on the lawn, motionless. How could the man just run into Vanessa's house like that? Newton wondered if he should call the police, but he didn't want to leave to find a telephone. Instead, he followed the man through the open front door, into the house, and up the stairs. Long before he reached the top he could hear the man pounding on Vanessa's door and yelling in a voice that Newton was sure could be heard for miles around.

"Come out of there this instant!" the man shouted. "I saw you go in the window, and I want you out here in the hall now. You're all going back with me! Do you hear me? You're going back with me!"

Newton peeked over the top stair into the hallway. "I know you're all in there!" shouted the man. "I'm going to count to ten, and I want that door open before I finish!"

Newton climbed to the top of the stairs.

"One!" roared the man. "Two!"

"Use the window," thought Newton.

"Three! . . . Four!"

"Fly away, Vanessa," Newton silently prayed.

"Five! . . . Six!"

"You still have time to escape," thought Newton.

"Seven! . . . Eight!"

"Go!" thought Newton.

"Nine!"

"Vanessa!"

The sound of Vanessa's name echoed and reverberated up and down the hall, and Newton realized to his amazement and utter dread that he had shouted her name out loud.

The man turned. His face was a mask of fury. He saw Newton and took a step toward him, and then . . .

Click!

It was the sound of the lock on Vanessa's door being unlatched. The man pivoted in one motion on the ball of his foot to face the door. Newton came up beside him.

The door opened slowly, and a figure stepped out.

It was Vanessa.

Newton stared for a moment. There was something different about her, but he couldn't tell what it was at first. Then he saw.

The wings. . . .

"They're gone!" whispered Newton.

Ruth Ann Harbinger stepped out into the hallway behind Vanessa. She had no wings, either.

One after another, the members of Newton's class at school stepped out of Vanessa's room. After a while it started to remind Newton of the old circus trick in which dozens of clowns climbed out of a tiny automobile. Soon the hallway was crowded with his fellow students.

None of them had wings.

Newton looked at Vanessa and caught her eye. His look said, "What happened?" and it seemed to him that she raised her eyebrows in a way that answered, "I'll tell you later."

The man in the black hat stood in the middle of all this. He looked at them all, one by one.

"I suppose you think you've been very clever," he said. "Very clever."

"I'm sure we don't know what you're talking about," cut in Vanessa.

"You know very well what I'm talking about!" roared the man. "The wings! I saw them with my own eyes, although I must have been blind not to see that you were involved, young lady!"

"And what would you have done if you'd known?" said Vanessa. "Would you have kept me trapped with all the rest of them in that cage so you could study us? Would you have stuck pins in us one by one, or dissected us to find out our innermost secrets? Or would you have sold tickets so that people could come and gawk at us like freaks in some fantastic crazy zoo? Or maybe you planned to sell us to the government as the ultimate secret weapon — things with wings."

The man stood there facing Vanessa, but she refused to look directly at him. His expression was hard to read behind the mirrored glasses.

"Vanessa," said the man. "Is that what you really think? That's not it at all."

"What is it, then?" asked Vanessa. "What great

plans do you have to bring you fortune and fame at our expense?"

"Vanessa, let me explain," said the man. "You, of all people, should understand. After all, you and I are scientists. We think the same way. We look at the world the same way. In many ways you and I are the same."

"We're not the same," said Vanessa. "We may both study things that fly, but I love them, and you don't even like them. How can you live that way?"

"Vanessa," said the man. "You don't understand. . . ."

"No," said Vanessa. "*You* don't understand. You never have, and you never will." She turned and walked back into her room, slamming the door behind her.

The man in the black hat stood looking at the closed door. He stood there a long time. Slowly, the crowd of students flowed around him and filed down the stairs, until only Newton remained. Newton started to follow the others down the stairs, but then he changed his mind, turned around, and approached the man.

"Who are you, anyway?" said Newton. "You've spied on us, followed us, put us in a cage . . . and now you've yelled at Vanessa in front of all her friends. What right do you have to do all that? Just exactly who do you think you are?"

At first, the man didn't appear to hear Newton. He just stood and stared at Vanessa's door as if his thoughts were far away. Then, slowly, he turned toward Newton. As he turned, he took off his glasses, and rubbed his closed eyes as if they hurt. Finally, his hand came away from his eyes, and he opened them and looked Newton full in the face.

It was the first time that Newton had seen the man's eyes. He was surprised to see that they were not the harsh glaring eyes he had expected. They were, quite simply, the saddest eyes that Newton had ever seen in his life.

The man looked startled for a moment, as if he were surprised to see that Newton was still there. He quickly put on his glasses. Then, he shook his head as if to clear it, and sighed.

When he spoke his voice was almost a whisper.

"I am Vanessa's father," he said.

27.
GROUNDED

Newton didn't know what he would find the next day when he rode his bike up Vanessa's driveway. He'd waited until after lunch to give her time to straighten things out with her father, but finally he could wait no longer. The last thing he expected to see was Vanessa and Ruth Ann sitting on the front porch steps, but there they were, sitting and talking as if it were any normal afternoon of spring vacation.

Newton set his bike down in the driveway and walked up to the steps. He opened his mouth to ask the question that he'd been wanting to ask for the last twelve hours: What happened to the wings? But before he could speak a single word, Vanessa answered.

"They fell off," she said. "On the way in the window. The tips brushed against the edge of the window, and they were gone. It's lucky it didn't happen when we were flying. I guess it's a little like losing your baby teeth — they don't last forever. I went down this morning to see if there was anything left, but they had turned to dust."

"Was it awful after everyone left?" Newton asked. "Was your father really angry?"

"No," said Vanessa. "He started to tell me that I was grounded, and that I was forbidden to go any farther than the front porch. But then I showed him the green powder I'd brought back from the garden. At first he just laughed, but when I told him how it worked, he got this puzzled look on his face and stopped talking. He took the powder away, and he hasn't said a word to me since."

"You gave him the green powder?"

"I had to. He probably wants to sell it and make a fortune."

Newton had noticed that Ruth Ann had been listening to this conversation with confusion in her eyes. Now she spoke up.

"What green powder are you talking about?" she asked.

"The flying powder," said Vanessa. "The green butterfly scales. The stuff that makes you fly."

"Is that what you think?" asked Ruth Ann. "You think the powder from the butterflies' wings made you fly?"

"Of course," said Vanessa.

"But that's not it at all!" said Ruth Ann. "It's not the green powder that makes you fly. It's the tree."

"What?" said Vanessa and Newton in unison.

"It's the tree," repeated Ruth Ann. "Didn't you go into the garden?"

"Yes."

"And didn't you find the butterfly tree?"

"Yes."

"And didn't you pick one of those weird fruit things off the tree?" continued Ruth Ann.

Vanessa fidgeted a little and looked sideways at Newton.

"Well . . . yes," she said.

"And didn't you take a bite of that fruit?"

There was silence for a moment. Then Newton shouted. "Vanessa, you promised! You said you wouldn't take a single bite."

"Well," said Vanessa, "that's true. I did say I

wouldn't take a single bite, and after I said it, I didn't take a bite. But before I said it, I'd already taken one, or maybe two, and . . ." Her voice trailed off, and she turned to Ruth Ann.

"But what do the tree and the fruit have to do with flying?" asked Vanessa.

"Don't you see?" said Ruth Ann. "Every year when the tree blooms, the blossoms send out a perfume that attracts the butterflies. The butterflies fly from blossom to blossom sipping the tree's nectar. Each time they rest on a blossom they get a little pollen on their wings, and they carry it to the next blossom. I imagine that something in the butterflies' wing scales mixes with the pollen and creates a strange chemical reaction in the tree. Over the years, the combination has developed into this special fruit."

Vanessa nodded her head slowly.

"Ruth Ann, that's a pretty good theory from someone who isn't even a scientist."

"Hey," said Ruth Ann. "You scientists need us artists to help you stay creative. You can't have science without a little art thrown in."

"There are still some things I don't understand," said Vanessa. "I've been studying the butterflies for years, but it looks like you and everyone in our class found the butterfly garden and the tree before I did."

Ruth Ann looked down at the ground. "You don't own the woods, Vanessa," she said. "After we had our fight, I got so mad at you I decided that maybe I could find where the butterflies go on my own, before they even arrived. I went walking in the woods in the rain. I didn't know what I was looking for, but then . . . well, I found the garden. I admit I told a few friends, and they told a few friends, and before I knew it, it seemed like everyone from our class was there. Then, last weekend, the fruit appeared, and it looks like everyone tried it. I didn't eat any in the garden, but I did take a piece home to sketch. It looked so tempting, I finally had to take a bite."

"I can't believe you told all your friends," said Vanessa. "You didn't tell anybody else about the garden, did you? Did you tell your mother?"

"I didn't tell my mother about the garden," said Ruth Ann.

Vanessa stood up.

"I just had a thought," she said. "My father's not stupid. It won't take him long to realize that the powder doesn't do anything. Sooner or later he'll figure out what the tree can do. And then I know exactly what he'll want to do. He'll want to take the tree apart leaf by leaf until he understands how it works. Then the tree will be gone, and the butterflies won't have a place to come back to anymore. The butterflies will never return to Angel Falls, and no one else will ever have a chance to get wings."

Vanessa paused for emphasis. Then she continued.

"We've got to protect the tree. We've got to go back to the garden. We have to climb that tree, get a piece of fruit, take out the seeds, and plant them somewhere safe so there will always be another tree."

Vanessa jumped off the steps and started running to the road. "Come on!" she called. "We don't have any time to waste."

Ruth Ann raced after her, but Newton didn't budge.

"Wait a minute!" he called after them.

Vanessa and Ruth Ann stopped and turned around.

"Just slow down," Newton said. "You lied to me, Vanessa. You said you wouldn't take a bite of that fruit, but you did. And that wasn't the first time you lied. Why didn't you tell me that the man in the black hat was your father?"

Vanessa took three steps forward, then stopped. She stood very straight.

"That man is not my father," she said.

28.

WHAT HAVE YOU EVER DONE?

Vanessa and Newton looked at each other for a long moment. Then Ruth Ann spoke.

"Vanessa, how can you say such a thing?" she said. "You know that isn't true."

Vanessa turned to Ruth Ann.

"How can he be my father?" she said. "There's no similarity between us at all. If he were really my father, he wouldn't just study butterflies, he'd like them, too. If he were really my father, he wouldn't have stopped talking to me and shut me out of his life. If he were really my father, he wouldn't have let my mother die."

Vanessa stood there for a long time without saying anything more. Then she turned back to Newton.

"I never lie," she said quietly. "I just don't always fill in the details."

"Vanessa, your father may not be as bad as you think," said Newton.

"How would you know?" she asked.

"I've seen his eyes," said Newton.

"No one has seen his eyes," said Vanessa. "Even I can't remember ever having seen his eyes."

Vanessa turned away and started walking back toward the road, but then she stopped and came back.

"Don't come with me," she said to Newton. "I don't need your help. I don't need anyone."

"Oh, stop it," said Newton. "You're always saying that. But everyone can use a little help now and then, even you. Why don't you just slow down once in a while instead of flying off in a million directions at once? Take some time to really look around you, and you might get a lot more done on your own."

"You're telling me how to get things done?" said Vanessa. "You're telling me? How would you know? You're a watcher, not a doer, Newton. Without me, you'd never do anything."

"All I'm saying," said Newton, "is slow down and open your eyes. You might find what you're looking for right in front of you."

"Oh great," said Vanessa. "Now you're starting to sound like Dorothy in *The Wizard of Oz* — the movie version. How many times do I have to tell you, life is not a movie. You're not going to find your heart's desire by sitting in your backyard and watching life go by. If you want to get something done, you have to go out there and pay the price. I gave up the most precious thing I owned — my book collection. What have you ever done, Newton? What have you given up? Nothing! Go home, Newton. I don't need you. No one needs you!"

"You just don't see," said Newton. "You just don't see."

But Vanessa had turned away again and was already walking to the end of the driveway. Ruth Ann followed her.

Newton could hear their voices as they started down the road.

And he could still hear their voices seconds later when a car screeched to a stop just out of sight of the driveway.

"You two are coming with me!" yelled a voice. "I've called a little meeting with the other parents, and we're going to put a halt to this flying non-sense once and for all! First, we're going to make a few stops in the car, and then we're going to the garden to deal with this tree of yours!"

Newton heard Vanessa cry out, "Ruth Ann, you said you didn't tell your mother about the garden!"

"I didn't tell her!" Ruth Ann yelled back. "When I tried to find where the butterflies go, it was rainy and cold. I couldn't find anything. I went home and told my mother, and she told me all about the garden and how to get there. I didn't tell her. She told me. Vanessa, our parents know all about it!"

Two car doors slammed, and Newton watched as the car driven by Ruth Ann's mother sped past the entrance to the driveway. The last thing he saw before it turned the corner was Vanessa's face staring at him out the back window.

He saw the look in her eyes, and in his mind he heard her voice as clearly as if she were speaking to him.

"What have *you* ever done, Newton? What have *you* given up?"

And he knew what he had to do.

29.
UP iN THE AiR

Newton knew what he had to do, and he didn't like it . . . but he was doing it anyway.

He was halfway up the butterfly tree in the middle of the garden. It was not a hard tree to climb, but climbing was all new to Newton, and he was afraid. His whole body felt chilled, and no matter how hard he tried, he couldn't stop his hands from shaking.

Slowly, he pushed his left hand up along the side of the tree and grabbed for another branch. He kept his eyes focused straight ahead on the bark that was about an inch away from his nose and tried not to look down.

He'd run all the way to the tree, but when he'd arrived he'd found nobody there. Instead, he'd seen that someone had piled up a huge stack of smaller fallen trees and branches, leaning them up all around the base of the tree, as if to make a wall to keep people away. He'd laughed to himself because rather than keeping him away, the barricade had formed a platform that he had scrambled up, past the branchless lower part of the tree and into the bottom branches.

Now here he was, his arms wrapped tight around the trunk, hugging it for dear life.

He began to move again, climbing slowly but steadily. He was surprised to find that the courage to try something new like this did not come in a sudden decision and a giant leap upward. It came slowly, one cautious inch at a time.

Newton turned his head slightly to gaze along the branches. He could see the bright green of the new leaves, the white of the blossoms, and everywhere the rainbow fluttering of the butterflies, but so far there was no fruit to be seen.

Perhaps higher. Once more he pushed his hands up the tree to grab another branch.

"I feel like a caterpillar, inching my way up this tree," he thought. He wondered what would happen when he found the fruit and held it in his hand. He knew he was supposed to take it back to Vanessa, but what if . . . what if . . .

A thought brushed through his mind like a butterfly. What if he took a bite?

"I'm probably the only person in the whole class who hasn't," he thought. It hadn't been fun being the only one left out of the adventure. On the other hand, he wasn't sure if he was really ready to fly.

"How will I know when I'm ready?" he wondered. His parents were always saying, "There's a time and place for everything," usually when they wanted to talk him out of doing something. But then they always added, "And everyone reaches those places in their own time." He still didn't know exactly what they meant by that. Right now he just wanted to know, "When will it be my time?"

He continued to climb and search — branch by branch, higher and higher up the tree, but there was still no fruit.

The higher he climbed, the more his hands shook. The more his hands shook, the more his knees shook. The more his knees shook, the more his whole body shook. He couldn't believe that he had gotten himself into this situation. Here he was risking his life, doing something that he'd never done before, that he was petrified of doing, that he must be crazy to be doing, and why?

The answer came to him even before he'd finished asking the question.

He was doing it because even though she'd yelled at him, Vanessa was his friend, and because as much as he didn't want to admit it, she was right — he was a watcher, and it was time to be a doer.

Besides, there was no one else who could do it.

He reached up for another branch, and his hand found only air. He looked up then and saw that he was at the top of the tree. His right hand searched through the leaves, and then his left hand searched, and each one came back empty.

It was then that Newton realized the truth.

His climb had been for nothing. There was no more fruit on the tree. Vanessa and the others had picked it all.

30.
DON'T LOOK DOWN

Newton clung to the tree trunk and held on tight. His quest had been a failure and now the hardest part was still ahead of him — or rather, below him. He had to get back down to the ground.

When he had started out he'd thought that climbing down would be the easiest part of this adventure, but now he found that the athletic effort and the mental strain of climbing up had practically worn him out. He didn't know if he had the strength even to hold on during the long climb down.

Newton decided that slowly but surely was still his best bet. He figured that even if he only managed to climb down at a rate of a foot or two an hour, he would still eventually make it to the ground even if it took all night and part of the next day. But first he decided to rest for a while and gather his strength.

It had taken Newton a long time to climb to the top of the tree. It was now late afternoon, and he noticed that the rest of the butterflies were returning home to the tree to sleep. All up and down the branches, butterflies were landing and folding their wings up together over their heads. There were soon so many of them, so close together, that the tree began to look as if it had been covered with overlapping rainbow-colored shingles.

Newton was just beginning to turn his attention away from the butterflies and back to thoughts of the climb down, when the sound of a car door slamming drifted up to him from far below. He shifted his eyes a little and looked down, but found that the leaves, blossoms, and butterflies blocked his view, and he couldn't see the ground.

"I suppose whoever's down there can't see me, either," he thought.

More car doors slammed.

Newton had been concentrating so hard on not falling that he had never heard the cars approach. Now it sounded as if there might be as many as thirty, moving into place in a circle around the tree.

He could hear voices now, too, bubbling up unclearly from below. One voice sounded angry. At first he couldn't tell what it was saying, and then it broke through loud and clear.

"To the tree!"

Newton had heard that voice before. It was Ruth Ann's mother.

The voices seemed to be moving closer to the tree, but then they stopped and fell silent. Far away in the distance, a new sound emerged. It was the sound of someone leaning on a car horn.

The sound grew louder, and then Newton could hear the car's motor and its wheels as it came closer. Finally, the car burst into the clearing and careened to a stop.

"What is going on here?" shouted a voice. Newton recognized this voice, too. He had heard it sound just like this once before.

It was Vanessa's father. "Whatever it is that you're about to do, I demand that you stop it immediately!" he shouted.

But Ruth Ann's mother's voice chimed in.

"You're in no position to make demands," she said. "Everyone has finally come around to my way of thinking. We've taken a vote. It's all of us parents against one of you. And besides . . . how *dare* you try to stop us? You, of all people, especially after what happened to Vanessa's mother, right here on this very spot!"

There was a pause. Newton waited for Vanessa's father to say something, but time passed, and there was no reply.

Then Ruth Ann's mother's voice cried again, "To the tree! To the tree!"

Newton still had no idea what was going on. He didn't want to look down, but he decided that one quick glance might not hurt. He pushed aside a small branch, but the leaves were still in the way.

He reached out a little farther.

Was that smoke he smelled? Was someone cooking something?

He reached out farther. . . .

And pushed aside the veil of leaves. Now he could see clearly. He looked down.

Below Newton, standing in a crowd, was a group of parents. He recognized them from school and around town. Scattered among them were the kids from school, the ones he'd helped rescue, the ones who'd had wings. Somehow, they looked helpless and cowed next to their parents.

Vanessa and Ruth Ann were there, too, standing together, at the back of the crowd.

In front of them all, blocking the way to the tree, and still wearing his black baseball hat and mirrored glasses, was Vanessa's father. Ruth Ann's mother stood face to face with him. She held a long blazing torch in her hand, and she had a wild look on her face as she waved the flame back and forth above her head. She reminded Newton of one of the townspeople in the movie *Frankenstein*, marching to the castle to destroy the monster.

"We are gathered here together," cried Ruth Ann's mother, "to put a stop to something dangerous — something that should have been nipped in the bud a long time ago. This tree must be destroyed."

She waved the torch one more time.

"To the tree!" she cried again.

Newton leaned forward as Mrs. Harbinger pushed past Vanessa's father and marched toward the tree. Newton looked at her torch, and that was when he realized that the pile of wood around the base of the tree was not a wall, was not a barricade, but was instead the kindling for a mammoth bonfire — a bonfire that would burn the tree to the ground along with everything in it.

"Stop!" Newton yelled as loudly as he could. But no one seemed to hear him.

"Stop!" he shouted again, waving his arms. He leaned even farther forward, hoping someone would see him. . . .

And then he was falling.

31.
I see you

Newton had heard people in movies say that their whole life had flashed before their eyes in the instant when they thought they were about to die.

Newton experienced something quite different. As he fell, it felt to him as if time were slowing down. Everything around him seemed to become part of a movie in slow motion. His eyesight was sharper than it had ever been before, and he found he could see the smallest detail at the farthest distance.

He saw Vanessa on the ground.

She was standing very still. He had never seen her stand so still before. He saw her face move slowly upward until she was looking straight at him. He had never noticed before that the color of her eyes was green.

She was the only one who seemed to realize what was happening to him. Her mouth opened slowly and began to form the shape of a word. No sound seemed to come out at first, and then after what felt like minutes, he heard it, an echoing cry that went on and on and on, breaking over his ears like waves on a beach:

"Newtonnnnn!"

All of this seemed to go on for hours, but it all happened in a split second, and then Vanessa was running forward in slow motion toward the tree.

The crowd of parents slowly parted as she ran through them. Her father held out his hand as if to say, "Slow down — what's going on?" but she brushed past him. The only one who didn't move was Ruth Ann's mother. She had stopped her march toward the tree and turned to face Vanessa. Now she stood squarely in Vanessa's way, waving her torch like a flaming sword.

Vanessa was moving with such purpose that Newton could see there was no way she could stop or turn aside. He could also see that Mrs. Harbinger had no intention of stepping out of the way.

Vanessa charged head-on, until it looked as if a collision was inevitable. Then, just as she reached the spot where Ruth Ann's mother was standing, Mrs. Harbinger reached down, pushed her blazing torch upright into the ground, then flung her arms open wide to catch Vanessa.

Newton saw both Vanessa and Mrs. Harbinger open their mouths to speak, and a moment later their words washed over him.

"I've got you!" yelled Mrs. Harbinger.

But Vanessa was looking up, straight and steady at Newton, and what she cried was, "Newton, I see you!"

Mrs. Harbinger closed her arms around Vanessa. . . .

But she grabbed only air, for with the words, "I see you," still reverberating through the late afternoon, Vanessa shot up over Mrs. Harbinger's head like a rocket and took off into the sky.

Vanessa was flying.

Without wings!

Up, up Vanessa flew toward the tree, and just as Newton came tumbling through the last branches, she caught him in her outstretched arms.

"I see you, Newton," he heard her whisper as she cradled him in her arms. "I see you."

And then, as Newton felt his sense of time rushing forward back to normal, she circled once around the tree and brought him gently to the ground in front of the startled onlookers.

32.
FILLING IN THE DETAILS

Newton tried to sit up, but Vanessa pushed him back down.

"You stay here and rest," she said. Then she whirled on Mrs. Harbinger.

"Stop this!" she yelled. "Stop it right now! Can't you see the danger you're causing?"

"There is danger here," said Mrs. Harbinger. "Only, I'm not causing it. It's the tree that's dangerous."

"Dangerous? Dangerous! That tree has been here for hundreds, maybe thousands of years.

We're the newcomers here. We're the ones who are dangerous."

"Vanessa," said Mrs. Harbinger. "That tree must be destroyed."

"The tree must not be destroyed!" replied Vanessa. "Don't you realize that the tree brings the butterflies to Angel Falls. If you destroy the tree, you destroy the butterflies' home, and you destroy Angel Falls, as well. Next year the butterflies won't have any place to return to. There won't be any more butterfly parades or butterfly sales days. There won't be any more butterflies in Angel Falls."

Newton listened as Vanessa spoke, but his eyes swept the crowd, and he could see that her words were not having the effect she intended.

All around, people were staring at Vanessa, but Newton could see by the look in their eyes that they were all thinking just one thing — she flew . . . and she doesn't have wings!

Mrs. Harbinger spoke again. "That tree will be destroyed today," she said. "There are things going on here that you don't understand. If you won't listen to me, then ask your father. I think it's time he explained things to you."

Vanessa's father stepped forward. He stood

there, silent for a moment. Then he began to speak in a low, soft, dreamy way, as if he were telling a bedtime story.

"It seems so long ago — the first time that I saw this garden. I remember it was spring, just like it is now, and I was just about your age, Vanessa.

"I was walking in the woods, and I remember that a butterfly landed on my shoulder. I brushed it away and it flew a little farther into the woods. Then it came back and landed on my shoulder again. Every time I brushed it away, it flew into the woods and returned, almost as if it wanted me to follow it. So I did.

"After a while, I came to an old crumbling stone wall. I thought at first that it was the ruins of an old mansion because I could see that it had once been quite tall, but after following the butterfly along it, I saw that it was the boundary wall of a very large and very old garden.

"Most of the wall had crumbled, but the remaining stones were so massive, I remember wondering where they'd come from, how they'd got here, how long had they been standing?

"The butterfly flew over the stones, and I followed after, and to make a long story short, I discovered the butterfly tree. And what a discovery it was — a tree that seemed to inhale and exhale butterflies with every passing breath of the wind. There it was, in the middle of the woods, in my hometown, and I was the only one who knew about it.

"At least, that was what I thought at first.

"I used to walk to the garden every afternoon and sit under the tree and just think. Every now and then I got the feeling that someone was watching me, and then one day I found out that someone *was* watching me. When I arrived at the tree that afternoon, there were two young women standing under it.

"'This is our tree,' they said. 'Go away.'

"'It's not your tree,' I said. 'I discovered it.'

"'We discovered it first,' they said.

"Finally, one of them added, 'Oh, let him stay if he wants.'

"The other one was furious at first, but we finally settled things when it turned out we were both interested in studying butterflies. Years later, I married her, Vanessa. That was your mother. The other one was her best friend."

Vanessa's father turned his head slightly.

"You *were* her best friend, weren't you, Gabriella?" he asked Ruth Ann's mother.

Mrs. Harbinger slowly nodded her head.

Vanessa's father continued.

"Somehow, a lot of other kids in town heard about the tree, too, and soon it felt like there were as many of us in the garden on any afternoon as there were butterflies.

"And then we began to get sick. Something was changing us. It was the fruit from the tree. We learned later that the tree blossoms every year, but it only bears fruit once a generation. It's a secret this town has managed to keep for years and years. You've seen what happens now, yourselves. We grew wings. We could fly!

"The wings didn't last long. Almost as quickly as they came, the wings fell off. But then we discovered something new. We didn't need the wings. We could still fly, even without them. Your mother and I knew we were different now forever, and we liked it."

"I didn't like it," whispered Mrs. Harbinger. "I never wanted to be different. I just wanted to be . . . the same."

"To our surprise," said Vanessa's father, "most of our friends felt the same way as Ruth Ann's mother. They didn't want to be different. I don't know if it was a lack of courage or a lack of imagination, or something else. They gradually forgot all about flying, and finally, they lost the ability to fly."

From his spot on the ground, Newton watched the parents standing silently nearby. He looked at their eyes, and he began to understand.

What Ruth Ann had said was true. Her mother had known all along. Many of the other parents had known, too. They'd gone through the exact same thing years before. They had been able to fly without wings, but they'd given it up. Newton could see an empty look in their eyes that seemed to be a sign of what they'd forgotten and what they'd lost. *This* was the secret of Angel Falls.

Vanessa's father continued. "Years went by. We grew up. I married Vanessa's mother. We became scientists and studied butterflies together. . . .

"Then, almost ten years ago, something happened. One night in the middle of a terrible storm, the tree was struck by lightning and caught fire. The burn marks were still there this morning when I looked.

"Vanessa, you were two years old. I had to stay at home and take care of you, but your mother rushed to the tree to help save it.

"The fire department had been called but hadn't

arrived yet when she got there, and she flew up into the air to try to save the tree and the butter-flies. Somehow, a spark must have blown into her clothes. They burst into a blaze, and then the wind from the storm caught her and she was falling . . . falling . . . and I wasn't there to save her. . . ."

A loud choking sob rose from Vanessa's father's throat. There was a pause that went on for several minutes. Then, in a broken voice, Vanessa's father continued.

"I must admit, a part of me died that day as well. And somehow, Vanessa, even as a child, you seemed to know what had happened. I still look at the drawing you made when you were a little older, and I wonder is this how a young child imagines an angel, or did you remember some-thing about your mother that you didn't under-stand. I know you blame me, and I still blame myself. I don't know if you'll ever forgive me. If only I had been there. . . .

"Just after your mother fell, it started to snow — an odd, wet, April snow. The snow put out the fire and the tree was saved.

"Vanessa, your mother had inherited some money, and after she died I used it to buy this part of the woods and to rebuild the old wall around the garden. When we were young, your mother used to call it Hesperides Garden because in Greek mythology that was where a tree with golden apples grew. So I had that name carved on the door. I kept the garden maintained as a sanctuary for butterflies because she loved them so, but I hoped that no one would ever be able to get inside."

Vanessa's father sighed.

"I guess the wall hasn't really worked too well," he said. "Every year a few children find their way into the garden, and they always seem to be from the class that's turning twelve. I used to believe that was a coincidence, but now I'm not so sure. I think maybe it's too difficult for the younger children to find their way to the garden, and the older ones are no longer interested."

He continued. "As I said before, the tree bears fruit only once a generation, but there's no way of telling exactly which year it will be. I began to worry about what might happen when the next 'change' came if no one was expecting it. The town helped me build the dome. Each spring, parents are notified where to bring their children if anything should 'happen.' When something did happen this year, one of the parents was always on duty to watch over the dome. And, of course, we always have a large selection of books so that you won't go hungry. We weren't trying to hurt you. We were trying to keep you from being hurt.

"Vanessa, in my grief over your mother's death, I threw myself into my work, and I shut you out of my life. Gradually, I learned to live with my sorrow, but when I finally started to reach out to you, I found to my dismay that it was too late. Now you've shut me out the same way I once shut you out.

"Vanessa, all I want to know now is this: Is it really too late? Have I lost you forever?"

33.
IT'S HAPPENING AGAIN

Newton had been watching Vanessa. She had stood very still while her father was talking, staring directly into his mirrored glasses as if she saw something there.

Now she spoke.

"Wait a minute," she said. "That was a nice speech, but something's missing. I don't understand the part about the books. When Newton and I got to the dome, there was no one on duty and all the caterpillars were starving. There weren't any books."

"But that's impossible!" said Vanessa's father.

"The books are one of the main reasons we built the dome. The modern home has very few books in it, but here we have plenty to go round. Ruth Ann's mother was on duty that day. She'll tell you about the books." He turned to Ruth Ann's mother, but she looked away.

"Maybe being different is all right for your child, but not for mine," said Mrs. Harbinger. "I hid the books. It's the tree that starts children changing, but it's the books that give them wings and make them want to fly. I didn't want Ruth Ann to change anymore. I didn't want her to be different. I didn't want her to fly away from me. So I hid the book boxes under the beds, and I went for a long walk in the garden to think things over. I thought if Ruth Ann didn't have the books, she might stay the same sweet baby girl I've always loved. I didn't mean to hurt her, or any of the others. . . . I just don't want her to change."

Mrs. Harbinger crossed her arms in defiance.

Vanessa had not moved. She was still standing there, looking into her father's glasses. As Newton watched, a strange expression passed over her face.

Vanessa gasped and took a step backward. Newton wondered what it was she had seen, but he never got the chance to ask because suddenly her father's glasses seemed to flash with fire. Newton didn't understand what was happening at first, but Vanessa seemed to know. She suddenly spun around.

"Look!" she called, and pointed to the tree.

And then Newton understood.

In the general confusion that had followed after Vanessa had flown up in the air, Mrs. Harbinger had forgotten about her torch. It had been standing upright in the ground, but then it had toppled over. The flame had spread to the pile of tinder that surrounded the tree. The wood had been soaked with gasoline and had instantly ignited. Now the base of the tree was engulfed in a wheel of fire that had been reflected in the mirror of Vanessa's father's glasses.

"Stand back!" someone yelled, as a tongue of flame leapt into the leaves of the tree.

"The butterflies!" screamed Vanessa. "The butterflies!"

Newton looked up into the tree. Every branch, twig, and stem was covered with butterflies, their wings folded up over their bodies. The butterflies did not move. Whether they were sound asleep, or paralyzed by fear, Newton didn't know.

"If I were still up there, I could do something," thought Newton. But there was no way anyone could get to the butterflies now. Except . . .

"Vanessa! Come back!" he heard her father call.

Even as Newton's eyes turned to Vanessa, she was already in the air, speeding upward toward the tree, arms flailing and swatting. A cloud of startled butterflies was swept from their perches and exploded into the sky. They were joined by more and more as Vanessa swooped from branch to branch, sweeping and shaking, trying to make the butterflies fly away from the tree.

From where Newton sat, it was an eerie sight. The fire was growing stronger and spreading into the topmost branches of the tree. The sun was setting, and it looked like not only the tree, but the entire sky was ablaze. Giant glowing sparks shot high into the air and blended with the mass of fluttering forms as Vanessa spun in and out of the flames, trying to rescue the butterflies. To Newton she seemed to be moving from light to shadow, shadow to light, as she circled the tree.

At first it looked as if she was sure to succeed, but some of the butterflies were stubborn and would not leave their home. After a while, Newton could see that Vanessa was tiring, and there was still one large branch that the butterflies would not leave.

Vanessa flew in for another try, but just then a white hot ember the size of a fist whizzed upward and struck her in the shoulder. She was knocked sideways through the air, and Newton saw to his horror that the sleeve of her shirt had caught fire.

Vanessa brushed at it, and then flew back toward the branch of butterflies, but the flame on her sleeve had not gone out. Suddenly it flared, and Vanessa let out a cry that seemed to come from deep inside her, a cry of pain and frustration and great loss.

Beside him, Newton heard Mrs. Harbinger whisper, "It's happening again."

And then a downdraft from the fire seemed to grab hold of Vanessa, and she was falling, like a child who has flown too close to the sun.

34.

AN ANGEL FALLS

A s Vanessa fell from the sky, the sound of her cry echoed down through the evening.

"Someone's got to do something!" yelled Newton. He started to stand, but a hand gripped his shoulder and pushed him back down.

Then, from right behind him, he heard a new cry, and it sounded just like Vanessa's, only it was a cry of longing and love and great regret. Newton turned to where the sound had come from, and he was just in time to see a dark form leap from the ground and hurtle into the air.

Up, up, up the form flew.

Down, down, down fell Vanessa.

And just when it seemed too late, just when it seemed that nothing could save Vanessa from a terrible, terrible fate, the form caught her in its arms, in the exact same way that Vanessa had caught Newton, and wrapped her in a huge bear hug, which immediately snuffed out the flames.

Newton could hear Ruth Ann's mother nearby on the ground saying, "I guess it's true what they say, the apple doesn't fall very far from the tree," and then Newton could see the face of the dark form who held Vanessa in his arms.

It was Vanessa's father.

The two of them did not return to earth, but rocketed onward and upward until they reached the last remaining branch of butterflies. Vanessa grabbed hold with both hands, and then her father let her go and flew up beside her.

Together, they began to pull downward on the branch. Slowly, it began to bend. Then, with one strong motion, they snapped it from the tree, flew it out and away from the flames, and floated it gently to earth.

By the time Newton reached Vanessa, a crowd had formed, and he had to push his way through. Vanessa was sitting on the ground. Beside her, with his arms wrapped tightly around her, was her father. He was crying softly into her hair. His tears were running down her forehead.

Vanessa turned slightly and looked straight at her father.

"Thank you," she said.

"I'm the one who has to thank you," said her father. "It's been a long time since I've flown. I was afraid I'd forgotten how. Thank you, Vanessa."

Someone called the fire department, and when they finally came, they did what they could, but it was too late to save the tree. Because the firemen were afraid that parts of the tree might still be hot enough to reignite and start a forest fire, they toppled what was left of it and cut it up into small sections.

As time went by, the people drifted away. Finally, Vanessa's father stood up and walked with Vanessa to his car. Newton followed behind with Ruth Ann and her mother. They watched as father and daughter drove away. Then Ruth Ann and her mother gave Newton a ride home.

To Newton's surprise, as soon as they all got into the car, the two totally ignored him and began arguing. They kept it up for the entire ride, and they were still at it when they dropped Newton off at his house. As they drove away, he could still hear them.

"Ruth Ann, I should never have told you about the garden. If I'd known that this would be the year . . ."

"But Mama, I liked flying. I want to fly some more!"

"No, and that's final!"

"But Vanessa can fly."

"Do you have to do everything that Vanessa does? I suppose if Vanessa jumped off the Empire State Building, you would, too."

"I would if I could fly," said Ruth Ann as the car drove out of sight.

35.
GOOD-BYE

Not long after the fire, Vanessa and her father left Angel Falls.

It all happened very quickly. Vanessa's father put their house up for sale. It sold almost immediately, and the day after that Newton found himself standing in Vanessa's driveway saying good-bye.

Vanessa stood by her father's car with her backpack in her hands. When she spoke there was a little waver in her voice.

"'If I have seen further it is by standing on the shoulders of giants,'" she said. "That's a famous saying from your namesake, Sir Isaac Newton. 'If I have flown, it's because you were there to help me.' That's a famous saying from me."

Then, to Newton's surprise, she handed him her backpack.

"It's a present," she said.

"But I didn't get you anything," Newton said.

"Newton Bellnap, you're always saying that. Don't you know you've already helped me get everything I always wanted?"

"And some things you didn't want," said Newton. "I don't think you liked being a caterpillar very much."

"It was all part of getting what I wanted," she said. "If you want to be a butterfly, you have to be a caterpillar first."

She showed him how to work the catch to open the backpack.

"Don't worry," she said. "It's not so heavy, anymore. I've tried to clean everything out. The only thing left inside is an envelope. Promise you won't open it until I'm gone."

She got in the car and rolled down the window. Her father started the engine.

"Vanessa, I've been meaning to ask you," said Newton. "Just night before the tree burned, when your father was telling us all about the garden — I saw you staring into his glasses for a long time. I wondered what you were looking at. Did you see something?"

Vanessa frowned. And then the frown slowly turned into a smile.

"I did see something," she said. "Those glasses are mirrors . . . I saw myself."

The car pulled out of the driveway. A moment later, she was gone.

Newton sat on the front steps of Vanessa's old house and opened the envelope. Inside were two folded pieces of paper. The first was a short note:

Dear Newton,

My father and I have started talking to each other. Things aren't perfect, but we've been getting along surprisingly well since all this happened.

I talk to him a little, and he listens. Then he talks to me a little, and I listen. He says he doesn't know how he's going to survive having a daughter who can fly, but then I remind him that he can fly, too. I didn't realize how sad he's been since my mother's death and how much he still misses her. We've been talking about a lot of things, especially about my mother, and I've decided that the name they gave me is the name I want to keep — Vanessa Atalanta.

Everyone needs a middle name. I hate to think of you going through life without one, and since I have one already, I am giving you my other one. You earned it. Your friend, Vanessa

Just in front of "Your friend," a new word had been squeezed in: "Love, Your friend, Vanessa."

Newton slowly unfolded the second piece of paper. In the center, hand-lettered in calligraphy with green ink, was a single word:

ADVENTURE

Newton carefully refolded both pieces of paper and returned them to the envelope. Then he placed them all in his shirt pocket — over his heart. He would keep them, he knew, forever.

EPILOGUE
THE BUTTERFLY DREAM

It was a warm, sunny afternoon, and Newton Bellnap was sitting under an apple tree in the middle of a field, fast asleep.

He was having the strangest dream.

In the dream, he was running across the field. On the other side was something he had to get to, but he couldn't see what it was.

He was running faster and faster when suddenly the ground ahead of him opened into a giant crevasse that looked as wide and deep as the Grand Canyon. There wasn't time to stop, and he went over the edge and found himself falling,

falling, falling, into a place that was gray and cold.

"Why do I feel like I've done this before?" he wondered. "Why don't I ever see it coming?"

Down, down, down he fell, until he was about to hit bottom.

"I'm going to crash," he thought, and just at that moment the dream began to change. A warm breeze swept past him, and he heard a girl's voice calling.

"You don't have to fall," said the voice. "Use your wings!"

Newton looked behind him, and there, attached to his shoulders, was a set of butterfly wings. They were paper-thin, but they were wide and strong. At the last minute, just before he hit the bottom, he stretched his arms open and the wings began to work.

Up, up, up he flew, along the canyon wall.

The wall had changed, too, or perhaps he just hadn't noticed before, but now he saw that it wasn't gray, but white with dark markings.

Higher he flew, up past the canyon rim, and then the canyon dropped away below him and he saw that it wasn't a canyon that he'd fallen into at all. It was the deep V-shaped valley of an open book.

He flew even higher, and now he saw that the book was in the hands of a boy — a boy who was sitting under an apple tree in the middle of a field.

"Who are you?" he called to the boy, but the boy didn't answer. He was fast asleep. Newton looked again . . . and that was when he saw that the boy was himself.

"Am I that boy, dreaming he is a butterfly?" he wondered. "Or am I a butterfly who is dreaming he is that boy?"

He didn't have time to think about an answer because he heard the girl's voice calling him again, from behind the sun.

"Catch, Newton!" he heard her say.

Up he flew toward the warmth of the sun, higher and higher, until he saw it wasn't the sun he was flying toward at all, but something else, hurtling toward him through the air.

It was a golden apple. . . .

And just at that moment something struck him on the head, and he opened his eyes.

Newton looked around, still half asleep.

He shook his head to clear it and realized he had a throbbing headache. He touched the top of his head. A giant bump was beginning to swell.

What had hit him on the head?

Newton looked down, but there was no apple on the ground beside him. There was nothing there at all.

"What a dream," he thought.

And then another thought crossed his mind.

"Was it *all* a dream — Vanessa, the butterflies, everything? Was it all a dream?"

He looked out at the field and the trees surrounding it. The grass and the leaves were no longer that bright, light, new spring green, but a darker, more mature color.

And then he remembered.

It was the first week of summer vacation. School was over. Vanessa was gone.

He thought back to that day a lifetime away when he'd first met Vanessa. He'd been sitting under this very tree, hoping that things would never change.

Well, everything had changed. Vanessa was gone. Spring was gone. The butterfly tree was gone. Even the butterflies were gone. No one knew if they'd come back again next year, but Newton sort of doubted it.

Everything had changed, Newton decided, except him. He felt as if he was exactly the same person he'd been at the start of spring vacation. He was still afraid of heights, and he still loved movies. He was even sitting under the same tree and having the same dream.

But was it the same dream, he wondered? He thought back over it. Something had changed — the ending was different. He had wings. But how had he gotten wings if he hadn't changed?

He picked up the book in his lap and stared at the title page. It was not Edgar Allan Poe. It was a book he had chosen for himself, *The Thirty-Nine Steps* by John Buchan. He'd stopped by the library to say thank you, and Jasmine Byrd, the librarian, had recommended it to him.

"You've seen the movie, now read the book," she'd said. "I think you'll like it."

And he did like it. He'd never imagined that he'd be sitting under a tree one day, reading a book that wasn't for school, and enjoying it. Maybe he had changed . . . a little. Could such a small thing change a dream?

He shoved his book back into the green backpack that Vanessa had given him. And as he did, his hand brushed against something that was wedged way back in the far corner of the pack. It took him a minute to pry it out.

The thing he held in his hand was dry and withered and shriveled. For an instant, Newton thought it might be the apple that Vanessa had dropped on his head that first day he'd met her, but on closer look this didn't look like an apple at all. It looked as if it had once been round, and golden, and fuzzy and . . .

He suddenly realized what it was.

It was the piece of fruit that Vanessa had picked from the butterfly tree. Her two bites were still visible. It must have fallen into the open pack, he thought, when she threw it down that first day in the garden.

He looked at it again. Too bad it was dry and withered. He might actually have tried to take a bite. Now all that was left was the wrinkled skin on the outside, and inside . . .

Newton stared at the object in his hand with a wild surmise.

Inside, there would be seeds.

He placed the fruit very carefully back in his pack. Then he stood, slung the pack over his shoulder, and started to walk. . . .

Back to the garden.

"Every body continues in its state of rest . . . unless it is compelled to change. . . ."

> — Sir Isaac Newton
> from *Mathematical Principles of Natural Philosophy. Laws of Motion, I*

"*All* that we see or seem
Is but a dream within a dream."

> — Edgar Allan Poe